ONE WHEEL DRIVE

Scot Gardner

www.pearsoned.co.nz

Pearson
a division of Pearson New Zealand Ltd
67 Apollo Drive, Rosedale, North Shore 0632, New Zealand

Associated companies throughout the world

© Pearson
First published by Pearson 2007
Reprinted 2009

ISBN 10: 1-86970-586-6
ISBN 13: 978-1-86970-586-2

Series Editor: Lucy Armour
Designed by Ruby-Anne Fenning
Illustrated by Vida Kelly

Text © Pearson

Published by Pearson
Printed in China by Bookbuilders

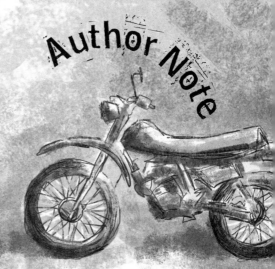

When I was young, I stole my dad's motorbike and went on a joy ride in the mountains. It wasn't the smartest thing I'd ever done, but I still remember the feeling of freedom that I found on those lonely roads. I made it home again — luckily — and my dad gave me one of those "I'm really disappointed in you" lectures when he eventually found out (they always find out). I've mostly grown up now, but I never got over motorbikes.

Scot Gardner

Mum had Caitlin by the wrist. I thought she was going to hit her. So did Caitlin. Mum had her hand drawn back, her palm open. Caitlin ducked her head and pulled away, trying to run from the lounge.

Mum lowered her slapping hand, her face red and ugly with rage. "If you touch Bradley again you'll be grounded until you are eighteen," she screamed. "Do you hear me?"

Caitlin's face was scrunched up like she was going to cry. "It was an accident! Yes, all right. Let me go!"

Mum dropped her wrist and Caitlin stormed from the room.

Mum stared at the hand she'd almost hit her daughter with, panting like a sheep that had been run to ground. She scowled at me, then stumped off along the hall and slammed her bedroom door.

I could hear Mum sobbing through the thin walls but I just sat there, shaking on the couch, and put my face in my hands. It was my fault. My family was falling apart and I was the one who'd taken out all the screws. Yes, I had a blood lip. It felt like I had a grape tucked against my gum. Yes, Caitlin had hit me in the arm. Well, it was more of a push. It caught me off balance and I smacked into the door frame. That's how I got the blood lip.

Mum had been in the kitchen talking to Dad on the phone. She swore and told Dad she had to go, slamming the phone down as I staggered in, howling and spitting blood into my hand.

"Brad? What happened?"

"Caitlin hit me and . . ." was all I said and Mum went off.

Lovely start to the school holidays.

Back at school, that Friday had felt like one of Dicky Quaid's over-pitched spin bowls. I was standing with my bat at the crease of life and I could see this lollipop of a delivery coming towards me, as if two weeks' holiday had been bowled underarm. I was going to smack it for six. The boys and I were going camping. Take the opportunity to go a bit feral. Catch a few fish, have a roaring campfire.

But now that school had finished and I was home, I felt as if I'd stuffed the shot. Taken a top edge and sent the ball straight into the air. Even if I apologised and told Mum the full story, Caitlin would never forgive me. With Mum working long hours it would be just Caitlin and me at home. She'd kill me the first chance she got. Or maybe she'd just torture me until I broke down.

Like Mum had.

Mum had never been aggro like that with Caitlin before. I'd noticed she'd been getting more and more cranky and dumping more jobs on me. I didn't mind the work. It got me out of the house. I'd buried a lamb that died in a frost and saved another that had become tangled in the bracken fern near the dam. I'd split nearly a year's worth of firewood in the last month and she still wasn't happy. Fridays were the worst. Getting up in the winter dark and coming home in the winter dark adds up during the week.

I crawled into bed at 9.35 and I could still hear

her sniffing. Two hours. Mum hadn't cried that long even when Pop died. She went to the toilet at ten and I heard her knock on Caitlin's door.

Mum's voice was barely a squeak. "Can I come in, love?"

Caitlin made some sort of response and the door opened and closed again. I heard them mumbling. I couldn't hear the words but it's amazing how much you can tell about a conversation by the tone of a voice. Mum's mumbles were pleading with Caitlin. Sounded like she was sorry.

Mum stuck her head into the hall. "Brad? You awake?"

I snorted and rolled over as if I wasn't wide awake and listening.

"Brad?"

"Wha?"

"You awake?"

Grumble, grumble.

"Can you come in here for a minute, love?"

I squinted against the light and rubbed my eyes. I yawned but my heart wasn't in it. In fact, my heart felt as if it needed a tune-up. It was idling at about five thousand revs. Way too fast.

I knew what Mum was going to tell us and it

was as if I'd been holding my breath since the last school holidays. Dad had been away working for three months. Three months I'd been going blue in the face waiting for this conversation.

"He's not coming back, is he?" I said.

"No!"

"I knew it. You and Dad are splitting up, aren't you?"

"No, Brad."

Caitlin snorted a laugh.

"Sit down. Shut up. Listen."

I crossed my arms and sat on the edge of Caitlin's bed.

"I'm sorry," Mum said. "I'm sorry I haven't been here for you guys. Sorry I've been at work so much and you've had to get yourselves up for the bus and then come home to an empty house at night. Sorry you've had to make so many of your own meals. Sorry my fuse has been . . . " She swallowed hard. "Sorry you guys have been copping it."

Her head dropped and I was thinking, yes, right . . . AND?

"Dad's coming home."

One of Caitlin's eyebrows shrugged as she

looked at me.

I sighed and three months of holding my breath came out with it. I felt like leaping off the bed and punching the air above my head. I felt like tearing around the house like a three-year-old, shouting, "Daddy's coming home! Daddy's coming home!" I felt like crying but I tend to keep tears for very special occasions. There was something about the way Mum's shoulders were hanging that wasn't quite right.

"Dad's coming home some time soon. Don't know when."

"What happened? Wasn't he supposed to be working until the end of the year?" Caitlin asked.

Mum nodded. "He's been working his backside off for three months. He and Vic and Carl and the others. They haven't paid him. They've been giving them beer money and promising them their proper pay next week. One more week. Now the station's gone bankrupt. Doesn't look like Dad's going to be paid at all. Three months' work down the drain!"

She shook her head and her whole body started rocking. "Three months! Means I'll be working at Gellerton stinking Cheese until I'm one hundred years old. Means we might have to move into town."

"What?" Caitlin's face lit up.

Mum nodded. "Means we might lose the farm."

I got up early on Saturday. Mum and Caitlin were still in bed when I pulled on my gumboots and went to check the sheep. I pushed through the gate at the back of the shed and frowned against the morning sun.

My breath was turning to puffs of fog and from horizon to horizon was a cloudless winter blue. But there was a thunderstorm in my head and I hated my sister more than ever. It's a special sort of hate I have for my big sister. It bubbles in my veins like acid. It makes the discomfort Mrs Fanshawe dishes out in English seem like a pleasure. It's bigger and hotter than the dislike I have for the kids who nicked my skateboard and busted the deck.

Caitlin actually wants to shift into town. She only comes out of the house in summer and only when it's hotter inside than it is outside. She hates the farm. She'd rather live in a flat in the middle of Gellerton. A short walk from the plaza. A short walk from Trinity, where Jordan Gray goes to school. A short walk from Jordan Gray's house so she wouldn't have to work up a sweat going to visit him.

I grew up in Woodridge. I've lived on Brandy Creek Road since I came home from the hospital. I love the paddocks and the little balls of sheep poop. All my good mates live out here and there are places to get lost and camp and fish and have a fire. We can go scrounging for treasure at the rubbish tip. They don't have rubbish police out here like they do at the Gellerton tip. I reckon I'd curl up and die if I had to live in town.

I walked to the eastern boundary that morning. Half an hour across the paddocks. I looked into the bush of the Brandy Creek Reserve and felt a tingle of excitement mixed in with all the yucky feelings about Caitlin and losing the farm.

Out of control. My life felt out of control. Except for Wednesday, when me and Wazza and Rick and the kid from Trinity who plays cricket with us, Huddo, were going bush. I only had to

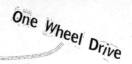
survive until Wednesday.

Mum and Caitlin were piling stuff into the Toyota when I got back. "Oh, there you are. We're going into town. You coming?" Mum asked.

Caitlin traced a love heart in the mud on the window. Mum unlocked the car and my sister dived into the passenger seat and slammed the door.

I shook my head. "I think I'll stay. Might go up the tip."

Mum rattled the keys in her hand and sighed. "Right. We'll be back soon."

She climbed behind the wheel, got out again, kissed me, said see you and drove off.

I've been staying at home on my own since I was ten. Maybe it's just what happens on farms. You're given more responsibilities so you end up more responsible. Some of the kids in my year at school still aren't allowed to stay at home by themselves.

But I didn't feel very responsible that Saturday. I felt like smashing something. The rubbish tip is always a good option when I'm feeling like that, but it wasn't the tip I needed that morning. I felt like trashing something of my sister's. I kicked my boots off at the back door.

My nose wrinkled as I pushed into Caitlin's room. Hairspray and deodorant made the air taste like metal. There was a wet towel on the floor, her pyjamas had been piled on her unmade bed and her top drawer was open.

There was a folded note tucked against the side of the drawer. It was a love note from Jordan, handwritten on a piece of lined A4. He'd almost filled the whole page with words. His writing was neat and rounded like a girl's but his spelling was really bad.

"I never thort I'd feel this way. When we are together my heart sings and I never want too let you go. Evrything seems briter when your with me."

I giggled and tried not to be sick. I folded the note carefully and put it back exactly as I'd found it. Then I picked up the Stephen King book on her dresser and shifted the bookmark three pages. It wasn't exactly trashing her room but it made me feel better for about a minute.

I pulled on my boots and stood in the oily cool of the machine shed. A magpie was scritching on the roof above me. It warbled a lazy morning call and I felt like a pervert. I shouldn't have gone into Caitlin's room. Mum is always going on about how we should respect each other's privacy and I know I'd flip if I found out Caitlin had been in my room. It was dumb to go into her room.

Mum knew Caitlin and Jordan were an item before they did. She said she could tell by the way Caitlin was being nice to me. Mum knew she was taking a big risk letting Caitlin go to the party. It was supposed to be supervised but Mum had her doubts. Dad wouldn't have let her go.

Caitlin even convinced Mum to let her take some of Dad's beer, saying that it was better that she took her own rather than drink what was on offer. Mum knew Caitlin had drunk more than the two cans of beer she'd given her. Mum picked her up from the couch at Jordan's place and she vomited in the car on the way home. She vomited all over her sheets and Mum banned her from seeing Jordan and grounded her for the rest of the year — until Dad got home and they could have a proper talk about it. Mum said she felt like she couldn't trust Caitlin and she'd been lied to.

Caitlin took it out on me as if it was my fault

she was grounded. She became the meanest dog in the world and I just kept out of her way. I should have kept out of her room.

There was a hessian bag stuffed full of wool on the machine shed workbench and I punched it. It was rounded like a belly and I punched it again. And again. It was soft as a body. I found a bit of rope and tied it to the top. Instant punching bag. All I had to do was loop the rope through one of the metal beams in the roof and hoist it off the floor.

I tried about twenty times to throw the rope through. No go. So I thought I'd climb one of the wall frames and monkey my way out. I looped the rope over my shoulder and jumped to the first handhold on the wall.

My fingers closed on something. Keys. Not house keys. I lowered myself to the ground and felt a rush of blood to my head as I realised what I had found. Change of plan. I unlooped the rope and stuffed the bag back on the bench. A mad smile hung on my lips as I moved the wheelbarrow, dragged the tarp off and slotted the key where it belonged: in the ignition of Dad's motorbike.

Dad's bike is nothing wild. Honda XL 185. An old road-trail four-stroke with knobby tyres. He uses it to yard the sheep and once, when I was ten, he tried to help me ride it. It was too heavy and I dropped it before I really got going. It freaked me out and I didn't want another go. He said he'd buy me a smaller bike one day but that was before he lost his job.

When the steel works closed down, Dad had to lean on his hobby — shearing — for money. Five guys from the steel works — Dad, Vic Wheelan, Carl Adderly and two guys I'd never met — had all done some shearing so they joined the union and hired themselves out as a team. They had their picture in the local paper and everything.

They got a little bit of work around home, then Vic landed a shearing job in Queensland through an employment agency. On a real station with thousands of sheep. He got in his ute and a week later phoned Dad to invite him up to sunny Queensland. Nine months' work for the whole team if they wanted it. One of the guys from the original steel works team got a full-time job at Gellerton Cheese so that left Dad and Carl and the other bloke. Jacko! Or maybe Jacko was the one who went to work at the cheese factory?

Anyhow, that was why I'd only spoken to Dad on the phone in the last three months. I missed our chess tournaments in front of the slow-combustion heater (I beat him for the first time ever last winter). I missed mucking around on the farm with him. I missed yarding the sheep: "the girls", as he calls them. His motorbike looked smaller and older than I remembered.

When we yard the sheep, Dad doubles me to the back of the mob and I do the legwork while he putters along and heads off any strays. Mum reckons we should get a kelpie but Dad says we don't have enough work for a real working dog.

"Besides," Dad said once, smiling at me, "how many working dogs do you know who can open gates?"

I'm built more like a greyhound than a kelpie but I like the legwork. "Go wide! Bring 'em in, Brad. Well done, mate. Yard 'em up." We dock the lambs' tails. Crutch the mob. Put little rings on the ball bags of the male lambs so they don't all turn out like Blinky.

Blinky is a stud merino ram but he's a bit past his prime. Dad paid $180 for him at the market and the first week he was living at our place he butted Dad in the leg and got me a beauty in the backside. I had a bruise as big as a tennis ball on my left cheek and Dad limped for a week. You've got to keep an eye on him when you're moving the mob. Dad's fairly safe from Blinky on the bike but sometimes I have to jump to the side at the last minute. I feel like a mini bullfighter when I manage to dodge old Blinky. Olé!

I sat on Dad's bike and the toes of my gumboots touched the ground on either side. I could hear petrol sloshing in the tank as I rocked the bike a bit. It was nearly full. I checked the oil. Fine. I turned the key. Nothing. No lights on the dash. Nothing. Flat battery.

Well, I thought, that stuffed that idea. I dusted the cobwebs off the dash and pretended I was riding. Then I decided to try and start it anyway and pulled out the kick-start lever and stood high on the foot pegs to see if I could balance on the stand. Easy. I held my breath and stomped on the lever. The bike lurched forward and I realised too late that I'd tried to start it while it was in gear. The stand clunked up and the bike toppled. There was an ugly crunch as the bike and I fell to the dusty floor of the shed.

I stood up and swore. My gumboot was stuck underneath the bike and I swore again as I tried to lift it. It barely moved. I could smell petrol and the panic that came with it powered me to heave with every muscle in my body. The front wheel slipped across the dirt floor and wedged against the leg of the wheelbarrow. But the bike was coming up. I felt like my eyes were going to pop out of my head. My arms were shaking, my knees were shaking and I panted through my teeth.

Suddenly the bike was upright and I kicked the stand down with my sock-covered toe. I put my hands on my hips and huffed. Nothing busted on the bike or me. I can do it, I thought. I can lift the bike if I need to.

I pulled my boot on and sat back on the seat,

holding the clutch and clicking through the gears with my foot. I rocked the bike back and forth in each gear until I'd found neutral. Well, it rolled freely so I thought it was in neutral. I held the clutch and booted the kick-start again. The engine turned over — blub blub — then died but the bike stayed upright.

Again. Blub blub. Once more. Blub blub. With every kick, a light on the dash flashed green. Neutral. Good. But why won't it . . . ? Choke! I found the choke knob near the speedo and pushed and twisted then pulled it and it clicked out. I kicked it again and the engine blurted before dying. One more kick and it barked into life. I revved and it roared. My arms were shaking and I thought I could really do some damage to myself. I could really get in trouble. And I could really have some fun!

I left the bike idling and ran to the carport to get my bike helmet. Mum and Caitlin had been gone about twenty minutes. They wouldn't even have made it to Gellerton in that time. Add half an hour for shopping and half an hour to get back and they were going to be another hour at least.

I strapped on my helmet, opened the gate

behind the shed and wheeled the bike into the paddock, closing the gate behind me. I found a gear and held my breath as I let the clutch out. It stalled. I started it again and pushed the choke button off. The bike purred and vibrated like a beast under my backside as I cranked the revs a bit higher. I let the clutch off, the engine laboured, then I was moving. Bumping along over the sheep-shorn grass with a smile on my face.

"Whooohooo!"

I stayed in the same gear and putt-putted to the Brandy Creek Reserve boundary of the farm. Blinky, the girls and all the new lambs stared then ran off in all directions as I rode through the mob. There was a raised patch of dirt behind the dam that had been trampled smooth by a couple of generations of lambs hunting for the highest point in the paddock to play. It looked like a perfect ramp.

I lined the bike up and I think I managed to get the front wheel off the ground as I rolled over it with the engine bawling. I found a higher gear and had another go. There was a definite bump as

I landed the second time and I smiled. It's just like a pushbike but you don't have to pedal, I thought. I'd been throwing my pushy around since I was five. Made jumps, ridden into the dam at the tip and worn tyres bald doing skids.

I started leaning into turns on the motorbike and powering through the gears. If I slammed on the foot brake I could get it to slide out like a BMX. I found that out by accident. And survived.

I stopped the bike at the pedestrian gate that Dad had made into the reserve. The tracks in the bush there go on forever. Wazza's always dreaming about the day when we all have motorbikes and can do some serious exploring. There aren't many tracks that we haven't walked or ridden our pushbikes on up there. Since Wazza has had the map we've been marking them off and adding details, such as the concrete slab near our campsite that Rick reckons used to be a jail and the blocked drain under the road that turned one of the little gullies into a lake.

This time of year we chuck our coats on and follow the streams that lead into Brandy Creek, hunting for good fishing holes and undiscovered waterfalls. Imagine how far we could get in a day if we all had motorbikes . . .

I thought about opening the gate. I had my hand resting on the chain but I wussed it. Mum will be home soon, I thought. There'll be other times if I don't get caught. I opened the throttle and roared back across the paddock to the shed. I wasn't Bradley Carstairs any more, I was Brad C, motocross champion and stunt rider.

I was buzzing when I finally took my helmet off. I put the bike back where I found it and pulled the tarp into place. I could hear the exhaust ticking as I leaned the barrow back against the tarp-covered lump and I could still smell exhaust smoke.

I'd just put the key back on the ledge when I heard the Toyota arriving and I scrambled up the wall with the rope. I was hanging by one arm from a rafter when Mum poked her head into the shed.

"What the heck are you doing?"

She startled me. She had a smile on her face.

"I'm hooking up a punching bag . . . Take out a bit of my aggro."

Mum nodded. "Good idea," she said. "I think I'll get some use out of it, too. Have you been up to the tip?"

"No. Maybe after lunch."

"We just saw Wazza and Rick on the road. Looked like they were heading out to the tip for a scrounge."

I left the punching bag swinging and rode my bike to the dump.

Wazza and Rick hadn't been there long. They greeted me with a smile through the smoky pong. Wazza was carrying my golf club. Rick had his arms full of empty aerosol cans.

The tip is another world. It's where we hang out. It's our shopping mall, but you don't have to pay for any bargains you find and nobody minds if you smash what's left. It's our BMX track, with ramps made of old car bonnets and a muddy dam to ghost into in the summer.

The tip has been burning since I can remember. It burns underground. Some weeks you can't see or smell the smoke and it seems like it has gone out but it's always burning somewhere. There are layers and layers of compacted rubbish down there and the fire brigade can't put it out. Sometimes in the summer the fire makes it above ground and into the forest along the boundary of the tip and the fire brigade have to come and put it out. They dump thousands and thousands of litres of water down the chimneys where they can see smoke but the tip keeps burning. It's like a dragon hiding underground. They'll never put it out.

We've never lit a fire at the tip. We'd get in trouble for that. But we don't think twice about feeding one that's already burning. A year or so ago we were hunting through the green plastic garbage bags when my foot disappeared down a hole. Wazza had to drag me out and when we looked where my foot had been it was all coals and bitter smoke and little flames. It looked like the gates of Hell.

The hole went down about three metres and it was hard to tell if what we could see was the bottom. We stared down that hole for a long time. It was Rick who imagined falling down there. It was Rick who suggested chucking something down. It was Rick who found the first empty aerosol, dumped it in the gates of Hell and made the first explosion. Now adding aerosols to flames is one of our favourite tip pastimes.

We do find treasure, too. Rick found a portable

CD player with batteries in it last year. He flicked it on to radio and it worked! We had music while we dug through the rubbish. We find disgusting things at times: maggoty food, bathroom rubbish, a dead dog. Wazza reckoned it had been a farmer's dog. Reckoned it had been shot for eating a lamb. Rick thought a car might have hit it. We dragged it down by the old car bodies and buried it using a rusty shovel with a broken handle. Rick made a cross from a broken umbrella.

My golf club is named Excalibur. It had a bent handle when I found it but it was fairly easy to straighten. It's a tool with a million uses at the tip: opening bags, smashing bottles and windows on the car wrecks. Oh, and popping old television screens. You haven't lived until you've smashed a TV screen. You have to hit them pretty hard and they sort of explode with a satisfying whump. And the glass goes everywhere.

You could hurt yourself at the tip. It wouldn't be hard. It's sort of dangerous, but so is walking across the street or paddling in the waves at the beach. We've had a few cuts and bruises and near misses. Rick splashed his hand with molten plastic when he was melting a headless doll. Nothing serious. We have to think about what we're doing. We have to be responsible. And have fun.

That morning, Wazza found a motorbike frame buried under some coils of rusty fencing wire. It still had wheels front and back but the tyres were flat. It still had a red plastic petrol tank. All it was missing was a seat. Oh, and a motor. He sat astride the frame.

"I've still got that lawn mower I found last year," Rick said. "We could use the motor from that. It still works. You could fix it up, Waz."

Wazza laughed, but not in a mean way. Wazza knew that anything was possible in his younger brother's mind. Rick is the biggest dreamer and he worships Waz. Reckons he can do anything with engines and electronics and that sort of thing. Although Rick and I were born only two months apart and there are three years between us and Wazza, I have always felt like Wazza and I are closer to the same age.

"We could, Rick. We could," Wazza said. "Might be a bit hard to get this frame home, though."

It was then that Rick noticed the flat tyres.

"I took my dad's motorbike for a spin this morning," I said.

"The XL?" Wazza asked.

I nodded.

"Cool," Rick said. "Does it go? Can you mono?"

"Yeah, it goes all right. I can only mono in first gear . . . and only for fifty metres or so. It's heavy. Really heavy."

And then I couldn't stop talking about the bike — how I'd jumped clear over a sheep, how I managed fifteen doughnuts on the grass before I hit power-band and almost rode into the dam.

"The XL's a four-stroke," Wazza said. "It doesn't have power-band."

"This one does," I lied. "Or maybe it just had a surge of power. Nearly flipped it."

"Right," said Wazza, unconvinced. He dropped the bike frame on the ground and kicked a can hard enough to send it clattering down to the car bodies.

"I nearly flipped the four-wheeler, didn't I, Waz?" Rick said.

"Yeah, but you're mad, Rick."

Rick and I laughed and I wished I'd told them the truth. Wished I didn't have to pretend that I'm a big hero.

It rained and hailed on Sunday. I got soaked first
thing while I was checking the sheep and when I
got back I showered until the hot water ran out.
Mum wasn't going to knock on the wall and tell
me I was wasting water; it was falling from the
sky ten times faster than it was going down the
plughole and the tanks were overflowing.

I played Cannibal Vortex on the PlayStation in
the morning and in the afternoon watched Carlton
mince the Bears. The Blues had a ten-goal lead by
half-time but I sat through the whole game.

Wazza phoned just after the footy finished. He
wanted to know if we were still going camping
even if it was raining.

"Yes, of course."

I could hear his brother shouting something in
the background.

"What did he say?" I asked.

"Said he's got a fishing rod for you."

Rick had borrowed one of my old rods and somehow got the tip caught in the spokes of his bike as he was riding home and snapped it. He'd been promising to replace it all year.

Caitlin stomped into the kitchen. "What were you doing in my room?"

I screwed up my face and shook my head.

"Rick said you could keep the rod he's got for you," Wazza said. "Replace the one he broke."

"Tell him not to worry about the busted one. It was falling apart."

Caitlin turned up her volume. "What were you doing in my stuff?"

I covered the mouthpiece. "I wasn't in your stuff. Why would I be?"

"You were in my room."

"Where's your evidence?"

"I . . . I just know."

"Could have been Mum," I said, my face getting hot.

"What was that?" Wazza asked.

"Bull," Caitlin barked as she stomped down the hall.

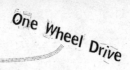

"Oh, nothing," I said into the phone. "Just dog breath going off at me again."

"Your mum?"

"No . . . Caitlin!"

Wazza told me about the stuff he was bringing but I hardly heard a word. There was a rat's nest in my stomach and I could feel my heart beating in my temples. That was close.

Mum was leaving for work when I got up on Monday. Her lips smacked on my forehead then she was out the door. I tucked the legs of my PJs into my boots and followed her out to the Toyota. She wound the window down and started the engine.

"Stay out of Caitlin's hair. Please," she said as she pulled on her seatbelt.

I huffed. "No worries about that."

"Why don't you ride down to Dale's place?"

"Huddo's in Melbourne with his mum. Won't be back until tomorrow."

Mum nodded. "Rick and Wazza?"

I shrugged then nodded. I'd made plans. If everything went smoothly, Caitlin wouldn't see me for the whole day.

Mum blew me a kiss then looked over her

shoulder and backed out of the carport. I waved and squeezed past the concrete water tank and had a pee on the lemon tree in the backyard. My pee made steam. The sky was overcast but it didn't look like rain. I could see a few patches of blue towards the coast.

I noticed the tree was loaded with lemons. It always seemed to have fruit on it. I can remember being taller than it. Now it touched the top of the water tank, fertilised by almost thirteen years' worth of Dad's and my urine. It's amazing we haven't killed it. Every night before I went to bed, as far back as I can remember, Dad and I would come out and pee on that poor tree. Sometimes we'd have a competition to see who could pee the highest and the furthest. Sometimes we'd just pee in silence and check out the night sky. I wondered how long it'd be until my next pee competition with Dad. Too long.

In Caitlin's window, all I could see were curtains. Eleven o'clock is an early morning for her during the holidays. I dressed and scoffed two bowls of cereal, emptied the books out of my school bag and quietly filled it with supplies. Two little bottles of Coke, a block of Gellerton cheese, an orange, two muesli bars and my pocket knife.

I was pulling the tarp off the bike when I remembered Dad's helmet. Full-face, with a plastic visor. Nobody would recognise me. I grabbed it from the laundry cupboard and wheeled the bike through the gate and one hundred big paces from the house. I didn't think Caitlin would hear it start from there.

I pulled out the choke and kicked it in the guts. Started first try. Untucking the straps of the helmet, I slipped it on my head. It was big but not huge and it smelled like my dad. I guessed he hadn't worn it for a year. He used to ride his bike to work in the summer occasionally. The helmet still smelled like his hair and his sweat.

I strapped it on and puttered past the boggle-eyed sheep on the far side of the paddock, heading for the gate that opened into the Brandy Creek Reserve. For a dreamy day of adventure. I looked over my shoulder at the house. Smoke swelled from the steel flue and hovered over the roof.

The visor fogged so I lifted it before unhooking the cold chain of the gate. Caitlin will get up, I thought, shower for half an hour, then go back to bed and read or maybe watch TV. If I rolled the bike the last hundred metres or so when I came back, she wouldn't see or hear anything. Her room and the lounge both face the opposite way. I pushed the bike through and set it on the stand while I locked the gate.

"Let's go," I mumbled into the helmet.

The bike felt supremely powerful as I rumbled through the bush. A freedom machine. The tracks were slippery where the tyres couldn't travel on grass and I sped up and slowed down to suit. The track I'd chosen snaked along the hill opposite the Brandy Creek Road. Where the bush opened up, I could see the white posts of the official road and, deep in the gully, flashes of silver reflected off the water.

I'd left the visor up and the air soon chilled my nose. The bush was alive with after-rain smells and I could hear lyrebirds calling over the sound of the engine. They're like a chicken with a long tail and a beautiful singing voice. They have calls of their own but in winter the males make mounds of dirt and leaves in the undergrowth and spend the days imitating the sounds of the bush − − a full orchestra of other birds' songs and strange noises. Wazza reckons he heard one making the sound of a chainsaw.

The track narrowed where a pile of rocks had fallen out of a cutting. I picked my way through the big stones on the remaining track and thought that a car could never get through there. Not even a four-wheel drive. I was in bike-only country. One-wheel drive terrain.

The track forked and I turned right. I should have turned left. The path got steeper and I changed down gears and dropped in and out of the rain-soaked channels that had carved up the surface.

A wallaby bolted across my path. I swore and stalled the bike. I pulled the clutch ready to start the bike again and it rolled backwards. My shin cracked against the foot peg, I lost balance and the bike and I both went down. With a crack.

My leg was under the bike. I could feel the heat of the exhaust pipe on my calf as I yanked and kicked until my leg came free. My gumboot was stuck under the bike again, only this time I could smell burning plastic.

With my sock in the wet grass I heaved on the handlebar and shoved the bike upright. The hill had made it easier to lift but now the engine wouldn't hold it. The back wheel and the motor turned and the bike began to chug-roll backwards down the hill. I swore again and shoved on the handlebar. The bike turned across the hill and stopped rolling. I couldn't put it up on the stand and I couldn't lay it down. My gumboot was out of reach and I couldn't let go of the bike.

I had to get to flat ground. I hooked my leg over the bike and pointed it down the hill, jamming so hard on the front brakes that my knuckles went white. Then I rolled and braked and skidded to the bottom of the hill. After I'd propped the bike on the stand, I managed to pull my hair getting the helmet off. Then I step-squelched the kilometre back to my gumboot.

A pattern from the exhaust had been melted into the ankle of the boot and I realised it was a scar that wouldn't heal until I got a new pair of boots. This was a scar that I'd have to explain. "I don't know how it got there. It must have happened while we were camping," I'd say. Or make up some other story.

The scar on my boot was nothing compared to the bike. The indicator was broken. The orange plastic had smashed when the bike fell over and it hung like it was going to fall off. I stomped my foot in frustration and looked up to the heavens. This was nothing like the adventure I'd dreamed of. How could I lie my way out of this?

On a damp boulder on the side of the track I drank a Coke and hacked at the cheese with my knife. I could ride the bike home right now and cover it up and act dumb. I could tell Dad that I didn't know how it happened. He might not even notice it. Well, not for a few days or a week or more after he got home. He'd notice it eventually. Dad doesn't miss stuff like that.

I started the bike and shoved the helmet back on my head. Then I pulled the broken plastic off the indicator and stuffed it in my pack. I thought maybe I could glue it back together again.

I rode quietly to the place where I should have turned left and followed the track across Merritt's Bridge and on to the Brandy Creek Road. I pointed the bike homeward and opened it up. The road was dirt but packed hard by all the cars that cut through the hills to the coast. I leaned into the corners and got into top gear near the old lime kilns. I had a smile on my face again.

It was a smile that only lasted a minute. There was a car coming the other way. A big white four-wheel drive with a bull bar. Just act cool, I thought. Wave as I go past. The car got closer and I died inside. It had too many lights. Lights on the bull bar and lights on the roof. Police! The headlights flashed and an arm reached out the window and waved me down.

I'm dead, I thought. It's all over. I'll go to jail and Mum will have to pay to get me out. Money that she and Dad don't have. They'll lose the farm for sure and it'll all be my fault. They'll shake their heads and never talk to me again. I couldn't believe I'd been so stupid. I'd known what I was doing. Mum and Dad were bound to ask questions. So why had I done it? I don't know. It was supposed to be fun.

I almost rammed a white post as I wobbled alongside the police car and stopped the bike. The policeman's face was familiar — the red cheeks and thick moustache — but he certainly didn't smile. I could feel my heart beating in my gums.

"Gidday," he said and grabbed a pad and pencil from the seat beside him. "Where are you headed?"

"Ah . . . home," I mumbled into the helmet.

"Pardon?"

"Home."

"Where's that?"

"Just . . . up the road. About five Ks or so."

"What's your name?"

I thought I could do it now. I could lie. I could tell him my name was Warren Turnbull but it'd be my luck that he'd know Wazza and then I'd be totally wrecked. And why would I want to get my friend into that sort of trouble anyway? Sometimes honesty is the only way to go.

"Bradley Carstairs."

He wrote it down. "You Leigh's boy?"

"Um, yes. Leigh's my dad. That's right."

"He still up in Queensland with Vic and Jacko?"

"Yes. Um . . . no, he's on his way back."

"Oh? I thought they had work until the end of the year."

"They did. The farm went broke. The one they were working on. They didn't get paid."

The cop looked at me. "You're joking?"

I shook my head.

"That's bad luck. More bad luck."

"Yes," I said and squeaked a laugh. "Bit rough."

"Your bike, Bradley?"

"No. It's my dad's. I've just . . . I've just borrowed it."

The cop nodded. "You're breaking the law. This is a public road."

"Am I? Is it?"

The cop frowned.

I bowed my head and nodded. It's all over, I thought. My heart was drumming in my neck.

"You seen anybody else in your travels today?"

I looked up the road. "Nope. Nobody. Pretty quiet. I haven't been on the road long. I came out near the lime kilns."

"Is that what those brick things are? On the left-hand side . . . just up here?"

I nodded.

"I thought it was part of an old house or something."

He was torturing me. I was busted fair and square and he was making me feel the pain. The engine under my backside ticked as it cooled. I could hear the creek splashing sharp against the rocks at the bottom of the gully.

The cop put the pad on the empty seat beside him. He looked in my eyes. Through my eyes. He was staring me down like Blinky the ram.

"Get off the road. Stay off the road. If you see these white posts, then you're breaking the law. You're not even allowed to ride on the side of the road. Hear me?"

"Yes."

He stroked his red-brown moustache and looked over his shoulder. "If you go straight home, you'll make it in time for lunch."

"Yes," I said and giggled like a preppie. That was it?

He started the car. "See you, Bradley. Give your dad my regards when you see him."

"Yes," I said and sighed. "Thanks."

He nodded and drove off. My whole body shivered but I wasn't cold. I fumbled with the kick-start and got the bike going. I looked over my shoulder at the back of the cop car then pulled on to the road. Never again, never again, I chanted. I turned at the first left and rode like a grandpa towards home. When I reached the gate I realised I had a campfire legend to tell Wazza and Rick and Huddo. I'd tell it exactly how it happened. How the cop took his gun out so I had to stop and how he frisked me and I gave him a false name and address.

I rode and rolled the bike back to the shed. The curtains were all closed. Caitlin was probably still in bed. The bike and I were freckled with orange mud but I wiped most of it off with a rag and covered the bike with the tarp. Then I glued the bits of the indicator back together and left it on the bench to dry.

When I was finished I punched and kicked the bag I'd hung from the rafter. It pulled against the rope and span, trying to get away, but I kept on pounding it. I thumped it until my knuckles were red and I lost a gumboot trying to drop it with a flying roundhouse kick. Landed on my backside in the dust. I flopped on my back and laughed out loud. I was still lying there chuckling when Caitlin walked into the shed.

"What are you doing, retard?"

I gagged and nearly swallowed my tongue. She was dressed. She wore jeans and her old black and white striped Woodridge footy jumper. She had her hair pulled back in a ponytail and I could smell her perfume from where I was sitting. She was outside. She was smiling.

"What's the matter with you?" I asked, sitting up quickly.

"What's the matter with me? You're the one lying on your back laughing like an idiot."

"Yeah but you're outside. It's daytime. It's probably not even midday."

"Shut up," she said and kicked dirt at me. I ducked.

She was still smiling. "I'm going for a walk."

"Where? What for? You only walk to the bus stop, remember? Anyway, you're grounded."

She shrugged. "It's a nice day. Holidays. Leave me alone."

Her feet crunched on the gravel drive, then she was gone. Out on to Brandy Creek Road and towards the Turnbull Reserve — the patch of grass beside the bridge that had been named after Rick and Wazza's great-grandad.

"Brad!" she shouted back.

I got up and hopped to the drive. "What?"

"Huddo phoned. He wants you to give him a call."

"Ohh. Okay. Thanks."

Something wasn't right. That was the most Caitlin and I had said to each other in a month and neither of us got hurt.

I pumped up the tyre on my pushbike and rode to Turnbull Reserve along Jackson's Track. I dumped my bike in the nettle on the side of the road and picked through to the fallen tree we use as a bridge across Brandy Creek.

Caitlin was nowhere in sight. I climbed the water tank stand beside the toilets but still couldn't see her. I shouldn't be so suspicious, I thought. I started talking to myself like the detective off *Sesame Street*. Sherlock Hemlock. He solves the dumbest mysteries — like the mystery of the pile of shoes beside the kindergarten door. Where did they come from? Who did they belong to? The door opens, the kids come pouring out and he pats himself on the back for solving yet another mystery.

Yes, well, I was about to solve the mystery of the walking sister. Why did she walk? Where did she walk? After ten minutes hanging from the tank stand I decided that she wasn't walking to the Turnbull Reserve. My arms were aching and as I climbed down someone on a mountain bike cruised into the park. I ran low — commando-style — to the toilets and watched the rider bump over the grass to the concrete pylons under the bridge.

"Aha!" I said to myself as the rider removed his helmet. Mystery solved. Jordan Gray. He must have ridden all the way from Gellerton. My hunch was correct. Caitlin was up to something. As I had suspected, it wasn't a little walk to stretch the legs. It was a secret meeting! Not so secret now, though, proving once again that I, Bradley Carstairs, am the world's greatest detective.

I realised, as Caitlin appeared on the bridge, that seeing through her lies was no great feat. My sister was not capable of an innocent walk down the road. She was sixteen and living in the country was not her ideal lifestyle. She wanted to be a party princess in the same way I wanted to be a motorcycle legend. I watched them hug and kiss then crossed the tree bridge before I was sick.

Eight

I'd forgotten that Huddo had phoned until he called again. I was sitting with Caitlin in front of the TV, pigging out on the chips Mum had bought for tea, when she hollered from the kitchen. I bolted and grabbed the phone, praying it would be a short conversation or Caitlin would eat all the chips.

"Hey, Huddo," I said. Puff puff.

"Brad!"

"You home already?"

"Yep. Do you want to go tomorrow instead of Wednesday?"

"Yeah, that'd be cool. I'll ask Mum."

Mum nearly nodded her head off when I put the question to her. If I wasn't home, Caitlin and I couldn't kill each other.

"Yep, that's fine. Will you ring Wazza and Rick?"

"Done. Going to meet us at Merritt's Bridge at ten."

"All organised."

"Yes. Don't worry about a thing, mate."

Caitlin had scoffed the chips. All that was left was the salty, fatty paper, stained with sauce.

"Thanks for leaving me some."

Caitlin nodded and stared at the telly. I screwed up the paper noisily and stuffed it in the fire.

I packed that night. I was in my pyjamas raiding the pantry, my arms full of packets of two-minute noodles and cans of beans, when the phone rang. I dropped them on the bench and grabbed the phone.

"Hello?"

"Gidday, Brad. How are you, mate?"

"Dad! I'm great. How you going? Mum said you were coming home."

"Yes. I'm on my way. But don't hold your breath. The ute's running like a wounded wombat so I've got it in for a service. I'm in New South Wales. Won't be long now."

"Cool."

The phone ticked quietly and neither of us said anything. I couldn't wipe the smile off my face.

"I'm sorry you didn't get paid for all the work you did," I said.

Dad groaned. "You and me both, Brad. What a waste of time that turned out to be."

There was another long silence.

"What you been up to?" he asked.

"Oh, nothing much. Going camping tomorrow with Wazza and Rick and Huddo."

"Excellent. Up the creek?"

"Yep. Usual spot."

"Had much rain?"

"Bit. It bucketed down the other day. The tank's overflowing."

"Really? It's as dry as a dead dingo in the desert up here. The drought's killing them. Even some of the bigger stations are going under."

"Yeah?"

"Bloody dustbowl. Nothing for the baa-baas to eat. Not a blade."

The phone beeped and clunked. "Listen, mate, I've nearly run out of change. Is your mum there?"

"Yes, hang on."

Mum ran to the phone. "Leigh?"

She said yes a few times, then no, and handed the phone back to me. "Talk to your dad for a minute."

She bolted along the hall.

"Dad?"

"Yes, mate. How are our baa-baas going? Mum says that you've been keeping an eye on them."

"Yes. Lost a few lambs. We had a frost a week ago and I found one snap-frozen near the dam."

"Really?"

"I buried it in the usual spot."

"Good lad. How are you off for firewood?"

"Heaps. I've split about a year's worth."

"Whaaaat?"

"I get a bit of a rhythm up and get a bit of aggro out. You know."

"Aggro? What've you got to be aggro about?"

"Ha! Heaps of stuff. Caitlin for a start."

"Mum said you two had been at each other's throats."

I swallowed. "Yes, we just . . . I don't know. Miss you. When are you going to be home?"

Dad sighed into the mouthpiece. "I don't know, mate."

Mum stormed into the kitchen carrying a piece

of green paper.

"Here's Mum. See you soon," I barked and handed her the phone.

"You got a pen, love?" Mum asked him and read him a number. Dad ran out of coins as he was reading it back to her and I struggled off to my room with my armload of food to finish my packing.

I was test-driving my backpack, walking up and down the hallway making sure nothing poked me in the back and it was all balanced, when Caitlin came out of the lounge and looked down her nose at me. "Going camping in your PJs. Very cool."

She shoved past into the kitchen. I heard her mumbling into the phone and I couldn't wait to be out of there.

Two-minute noodles are the perfect camping food. Thirty individual meals don't weigh as much as my sleeping bag and, if we all forgot matches (like last winter) or we couldn't get a fire going, I could eat them raw. If you've got plenty of drink handy, you can even eat the flavour sachet raw. Bit salty, but it's doable.

The sky clouded over some time during the night and I thought, as I bumped through the gate into the reserve, that it might be a raw noodle sort of camp. Unless, miracle of miracles, we found some dry wood. Not very likely. Big droplets from the trees drummed on the hood of my coat. At my feet, a fresh horseshoe print had made a tiny U-shaped dam. The dam was full. Even the air I was breathing was wet. I hoped Huddo remembered his gas stove.

Wazza and Rick were at the bridge when I got there. They had their packs covered with army-green garbage bags. Wazza had the collar of his oilskin pulled hard against his neck and his wide-brimmed Akubra hat made him look like a serious stockman leaning against the bridge rail. Rick didn't have a coat. The hair that poked out from under his tattered cap had curled damp around his ears so he looked like a girl from the back.

They hadn't heard me so I unleashed a double gumboot puddle stomp where the road meets the bridge. Some of the brown water splashed as far as Rick and he called me a loser but couldn't stop laughing.

"Loser? I just jumped in a puddle but I'm not as wet as you," I said and he shrugged.

"What time is it?" Rick asked.

I showed him my bare wrist. "So no sign of Huddo?"

"No, the big nancy boy. What's the bet his mum drives him?" Wazza said.

"What's the bet his mum doesn't let him come?" Rick said.

Wazza grunted and squeezed his voice box so he sounded like Mrs Hudson. "Now, Dale, I don't want you out in this. You remember what happened last time you got wet outside? Yes, you got that nasty bout of diarrhoea. We can't have you pooing all over your nice clean sheets, now can we?"

We hadn't finished laughing when a red Land Rover appeared. It sloshed along the road towards us and Rick pointed with his mouth open in a breathless laugh. "Huddo!"

Mrs Hudson waved through the windscreen and stopped before the bridge. The passenger door swung open.

"Can you move forward a bit? You parked right over a puddle," Huddo said to his mum.

She moved the car on to the bridge and Huddo dropped out, pulling his pack after him. He wore a fluorescent yellow cycling jacket that made me squint.

"Nice camouflage," Rick grumbled.

I smiled and shrugged. They were the kind of camping clothes only Dale Hudson would wear. The Nikes on his feet looked brand new. White socks. I looked at my melted gumboot and shook my head. Huddo the fashion-conscious camper.

"What happened to your boot?" Rick asked.

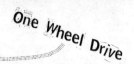

"Melted on the exhaust pipe of the motorbike."

"Motorbike?" Huddo growled.

Mrs Hudson backed and pointed the car the way she had come, waving as she went. We waved back. Except Huddo. He was pulling a black beanie over his ears. "Whose motorbike?" he asked.

"Mine . . . well, my dad's."

"You been riding it?"

I nodded and told them the story of my run-in with the cop. It wasn't outright bull but I did stretch it a little bit. No, I pumped it up to the max and by the end of it they were dead quiet.

"Go get it," Huddo suggested.

"No. I don't think so."

"Yes," Rick said. "We'll wait for you. You can teach us. I've never ridden a two-wheeler."

"It's just like the four-wheeler, Rick," Wazza said. "Only it's one-wheel drive."

"Go get it," Huddo said again.

"No, my old man will kill me."

Huddo scoffed. "And he won't kill you already when the cop does his report? How are you going to pay the fine? From your own money?"

"No, well . . . I gave him a false name and address, remember? He won't be able to . . ."

"What about the number plate on the bike?" Wazza asked. "He'd just put it in the computer and your dad's name will come up."

It was getting out of control. The story I'd told had painted me in much more trouble than I really was. Unless the cop told Dad I'd been on his bike, he'd never know.

"Yes," Huddo said. "You can double us to the campsite. Save walking."

"Good idea," Wazza added, rolling his eyes.

"Come on," Huddo said and looked at his hands. "We're getting drowned. We could set up our tents before the campsite was totally soaked."

They were dumb reasons. They were dumb Huddo reasons for getting the bike but they sparked a train of thought in me that made me take my pack off. Caitlin would still be in bed. Mum had left hours ago. Dad would be home in a few days or so and the opportunity might not come up again.

Huddo punched the air as I stepped past him.

I'd rolled the bike into the paddock and halfway to the gate when I remembered Dad's helmet.

I'd put it back in the laundry cupboard. I propped the bike on the stand, jogged to the carport and opened the flywire door. A mountain bike was resting against the wall, water dripping from its wheels, making dark patches in the sand. Jordan's bike.

I could feel the pulse in my fingers as I eased the door open. I grabbed the helmet and froze when I heard laughter coming from inside the house. Caitlin laughing. I'd almost forgotten what it sounded like. More laughter. Jordan's deep laugh. I sighed and shook my head as I crept back out the door.

I pulled the helmet on as I splashed across the paddock to the bike. The rain was chilling my backside through my jeans but the bike started second kick and I skidded, slipped and rolled to where I'd left my friends.

They'd gone and taken my pack with them. I crossed the bridge, heading along the Brandy Creek Road towards the campsite.

Squealing and whistling.

I slowed and U-turned, managing to stall the bike as the guys clambered out from under the bridge. Wazza had his pack on his back and mine looped over one arm. Huddo was still shouting and waving. He insisted on being first passenger.

"Just take me to the track. I'll walk down the hill," he shouted.

I kicked the bike into action and Huddo found the foot pegs on the back. The springs sagged with his extra weight and I stalled at my first attempt. Stalled at my second attempt.

"Come on, Brad, let's go!"

"Shut up."

I clicked down a few gears and tried again, revving hard and dropping the clutch. My helmet smacked back into Huddo's face as the front wheel lurched off the ground and the three of us — me, the bike and Huddo — formed a pile in the middle of the road. Bike on top, engine squealing, back wheel spinning like a giant weed trimmer.

"You all right?" Wazza asked, as he pulled Huddo clear.

I dragged my foot from under the bike, leaving a boot behind yet again, and grabbed the clutch. Rick helped me get the thing upright. He held my boot still while I folded the leg of my jeans around my ankle and slipped it back on. I didn't let go of the clutch the whole time. The engine purred.

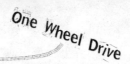

Huddo's nose was bleeding. His fluoro top was dashed with red like he'd just lost at paintball. He held the bridge of his nose and groaned.

"Sorry, Huddo. This wasn't a good idea," I said.

"No. Done worry aboud id," Huddo said. "Led me drive."

"No way," I said. "I'm taking it home."

"No . . . come on. Come on," Huddo said and shook his head. "See, it's stopped bleeding and everything. One more try."

He'd climbed on before I could take off. "Go easy on the clutch. Revs. Whatever. Just go easy."

I relaxed and pushed us along with my feet, then we were cruising and the brothers behind us were clapping and cheering. I changed up a gear, smoothly as you like, and smiled.

The hour of walking to the campsite turned out to be a ten-minute ride. I dropped Huddo at the top of the track and cranked it up on the way back to the bridge. Rick was next. I hardly felt him climb on. If I'm built like a greyhound, then he's built like a whippet. The bike was easier to ride with him on the back and he thanked me for the lift as he stepped off at the top of the track.

Wazza hung on like a koala in a hurricane. I

58

could feel his nails digging into my hips. He kept telling me to slow down. I stayed in second gear all the way. He was panting as his feet found firm ground again.

"That was awesome. Thanks," he said.

I revved hard and span dirt at him as I took off to get my pack. When I arrived at the turn-off again I pointed the bike down the hill and rode it straight into camp.

Huddo's dome tent was already up — with Huddo inside. Wazza helped Rick with the green and silver flysheet for the tent they shared and I felt like riding home. Everything was wet and getting wetter. The creek bawled over rocks in the darkened gully behind Huddo's tent. The rain slapped on the leaves overhead and thunked in heavy drops on the thin nylon. If it stopped raining that instant, water would still have been dropping from the leaves two days later. I couldn't be bothered putting up my tent. I couldn't be bothered opening my pack. I couldn't get the bike to stand so I leaned it against a blackwood tree and prayed that it wouldn't fall.

"Huddo, can I share your tent?" I asked.

"Yeah. No worries. Just wait a second."

Huddo's head popped through the zip on the door and he looked like he was hatching as he wriggled free. He'd metamorphosed into a new, clean and blood-free Huddo. A completely new set of clothes. He'd only been there half an hour.

"I sleep on the left side. You can have the right."

I pushed my pack in under the fly. He'd spread his stuff everywhere. There was no left or right in the tent, just a pile in the middle. I heaved my pack on top of it and closed the zip as I stepped out into the clearing again. The guys were watching me and smiling.

"What?"

They looked at each another.

"We're crazy," Huddo said. He turned his face to the heavy grey sky and shouted. "Toootally crazy."

Rick and Wazza chuckled and a smile creased my lips. Yes, mad as frogs in a frypan.

Huddo wandered down the track to the creek, his common sense in neutral, clapping his hands and rubbing them together. "Right, let's get a rip-roaring fire going."

Wazza and Rick and I went up the hill into the shade of the big cypress tree that marked the turn-off. There were patches of dry earth under the big tree and the branches we found were light and brittle. Rick spotted a dead wattle further up the hill and in ten minutes had dragged the whole lot into camp. Huddo found one wet log as thick as his arm. Fungi had turned the side of it orange.

"Bring any paper?" Wazza asked.

"No, I'll get some bark," Rick said.

"I've got some tissues," Huddo said.

"Tissues?"

"Yeah."

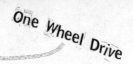

"You bring tissues camping?"

"Yes, why not?"

Wazza covered a nostril and blew. A glob of snot wheeled out of his nose and splashed on the grass. He swapped nostrils and blew again, then wiped his nose on his sleeve and smiled. "I always carry a hankie."

Rick laughed. "Yes, farmer's hankie."

"That's feral," Huddo moaned.

We lit the fire with bark and tissues. It flickered and glowed and I got dizzy blowing on embers.

"Here," Huddo said. "Give us a go."

He pulled a can of deodorant from his pocket and sprayed it on the tiny flame. It ignited with a paf and I rolled away through the wet grass. The gas roared as it burned, throwing flames and perfume stink deep into the pile of kindling. Half a can later, the kindling was a ball of flames.

Huddo smiled and showed too many teeth. "Must be lunchtime."

He disappeared into the tent and came out with two foam packs of meat — sausages and hamburgers — only he'd forgotten to pack something to cook them in. I fished out the little frying pan from the top of my pack. Huddo poked it into the bright flames and loaded it with meat. Too hot, too fast, I thought. The sausages stuck to the pan and the burgers turned black. He handed the burgers around and told us they were done. Black on the outside and blood red in the middle.

"Medium rare. That's the best," Huddo said.

There was a layer between the charcoal and the raw meat that I scraped off with my teeth and sucked down. I chucked the rest in the fire and told Huddo they were great.

Huddo dug into the tent and pulled out a four-pack of Coke. I leaned against the wet seat of the motorbike, thanked Huddo and opened my can. Rick and Wazza touched cans and said cheers. They'd pulled a log over to the fire and had to sit close to each other to stop it from rocking.

As they took their first sip, they burped, then ahhed in perfect sync. They're the exact opposite of my sister and me, I thought. They're brothers and good mates. Caitlin and I together were a recipe for murder.

I thought about Caitlin and Jordan giggling alone in the house and I nearly brought up my burger. If Mum finds out, she'll cop it big time. How did she know I wasn't out in the shed or

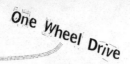

down the back with the sheep?

I rested my can on the wet bike seat and realised that I was a lot like my sister. The risks she liked to take had two legs. My risk was one-wheel drive. I also realised that she must have known we were going camping. Must have been listening when I asked Mum. She'd made her own plans. She may have watched me leave on the bike.

There was splashing in the creek then the clip-clop sound of hoof on stone.

"Someone's coming," Wazza whispered. Rick stood as a horseman rode into the clearing. Wazza backed against a tree.

The black horse was steaming and flecked with foamy sweat. The bit rattled in its mouth as it shook its head. The rider wore a dark oilskin coat and an Akubra like Wazza's. His eyes shone wide as he glanced around the camp.

"Gidday, fellas," the man said. His voice boomed and I realised my fingers had curled into fists.

"Gidday," Huddo squeaked.

"You guys seen a girl on a horse? Young girl on a big brown and white mare?"

We looked at each other and shook our heads.

"She lost?" Huddo asked.

Der, I thought.

"Yes, she's lost. Went this morning before the sun came up. Left us a note to say she'd be back at lunchtime."

"She came up this way?" Huddo asked.

"Yes. Merritt's Bridge."

"We've been up here since this morning and we haven't heard or seen anyone," I said.

"What's her name?" Huddo asked.

"Amber. Amber Jackson."

"Oh yes, I know her. She goes on my bus," Huddo said.

"You go to Trinity?"

"Yeah, I do. I know Amber."

"I'd better keep moving. If you see her, tell her to stay put. I'll call through on my way back."

"No worries," Huddo said. "Good luck."

"Ta," the man said and kicked his horse. It grunted then burst into activity, spraying mud from its hooves as it thundered up the track.

"Nice day to get lost," Rick said.

"Yeah," Huddo whispered. "And I don't like his chances of finding her. Amber's retarded or something."

"Really?" Wazza said.

Huddo nodded. "She sits right up the front and you can hear her talking like a seal from the back seat."

I walked across the track. There was a little U-shaped puddle at my feet, a puddle that had formed in the print of a horseshoe in the orange clay. That print set my mind on fire. I'd seen one the same that morning only it was miles from Merritt's Bridge. It was at our gate.

I put Dad's helmet on and swiped water off the bike seat with my hand.

"What are you doing, Brad?" Wazza asked.

I pulled the choke and kicked the bike into life.

"Brad?"

"I think I know where the girl is."

Huddo scoffed. "Yeah, right."

"If I'm not back by dark, you can eat everything in my pack."

Huddo's eyebrows jumped. "Cool!"

"Share it," Rick barked.

"Yes, share it out."

I revved and let the clutch out slowly.

"Brad!" Huddo shouted.

"What?"

"Can I have your can?"

He pointed at the Coke I'd left near the tree. I

waved my hand at him and skidded and slipped
up to the Brandy Creek Road.

It had started raining seriously by the time I made
it to Merritt's Bridge. It couldn't have been much
later than three o'clock but the clouds were like
a heavy curtain over the sun. I pulled the visor
down and found the switch for the headlight.
High beam. Rain splashed down my neck and my
fingers felt like they needed an oil . . . with nice
warm oil. Changing gears was a big effort. The
track to the gate had become an orange mudslide
and I bumped and slid along in first gear.

There it was. Creased in the clay near the gate
was a clear horseshoe print. It was fresh and stood
out against the studded mess of motorbike tyre
tracks I'd made. It wasn't alone and the trail led
along the hill to the landslip. Right into one-
wheel drive territory. Right up the hill where I'd
dropped the bike.

I sat at the bottom of the hill and revved the
engine. I thought I could ride the track that snaked
around the hillside to the right instead of the one
in front of me. But it would probably take another

hour and leave me searching for hoof prints in the dark. That would be wimping it.

Or I could follow the hoof marks that charged up the side of the hill. They had cut clean cups in the orange mud, as if they'd taken the hill at a trot. I turned the bike and for a second I was riding home. For just a breath I was going back to tuck the bike up in the shed and shower until the hot water ran out. Sit by the fire until my fingers thawed. Warm my toes while the girl on the horse . . .

She must be freaking out up there.

The front wheel slipped as I turned the bike but I caught it, pointed it towards the hill and gave it heaps. Mud spattered the back of Dad's helmet as I flew at the hill. The engine bawled and I dodged the ruts. If I stopped, I'd never start again.

The hill got steeper and the trees met over the track. The visor fogged and I snapped it back off my face, the cold air making my eyes water. It went on forever, that hill. My feet never found the foot pegs. They pushed off the ground and kept me upright. I felt like I was running with the bike underneath me.

The back wheel slid into a water-filled rut and

started to lose traction. I shifted my weight and the wheel bit at the ground, powering me out of the rut and popping a little mono. I rocked forward, the front wheel thudded to the ground and I wobbled on to smooth track. Ahead, the canopy opened like the end of a tunnel and the track seemed to vanish into the trees.

I ducked a low branch but it caught the visor and I heard the plastic crack. I swore as I crested the hill, braked and stalled on a smooth, flat track. I'd made it. I dug the heels of my boots into the soft ground and punched the air with both hands.

As I flexed my cold fingers and blew on them, I looked closely at the ground around me. Hoof prints peppered the mud beneath my gumboots. They went in every direction: towards the hill I'd just climbed, to the left track and to the right. She was confused, I thought. She didn't know which way to go — left or right. There had been only one set of tracks at the bottom of the hill so she hadn't gone back down.

Left. Right. Left? Right? Left! I started the bike and rumbled along the left track, scanning the ground for hoof prints. Twenty metres from the top of the hill, the confused mess of tracks died away. Only one set of prints remained. They were heading in the right direction, I thought. Down to the creek and Merritt's Bridge.

I found another landslide where a cutting had tumbled across the track. There was only room for a bike . . . or a horse. I bumped over loose stones and for a moment came close to the edge, my right foot pushing over rocks, my left kicking into thin air. I didn't look. The hillside seemed to drop through the trees straight into the creek, two hundred metres below.

I held my breath until I'd passed the landslip then rode on for a minute before I realised I'd lost the trail I'd been following. I stopped the bike and propped it on the stand. The rain ticked heavily on the helmet as I scanned the track for prints, working my way back on foot to the landslip. I felt my chest cave in as I realised the tracks I'd been following disappeared at the landslip.

"No," I whispered and my breath froze in my throat. I dropped to my knees and looked over the edge.

Through the trees, perhaps thirty metres from the road, I could see the upturned belly of a horse. A rainbow-coloured girth strap cut across its chest and a foreleg pointed at the sky. It wasn't moving.

I didn't think. I heaved myself over the edge and went sliding down the hill on my backside, shouting and swearing. I slid to a stop against the horse's wet brown belly but there was no response. I scrambled not to touch it and tumbled against it anyway. It was still warm.

"Hello? Hello! Please . . ." I shouted.

The rain fell heavily on the helmet. I tried to rip it off but my cold fingers refused to cooperate. I couldn't grip the strap properly.

"Hello?"

I stood wedged against the horse's belly and looked through the trees further down the hill. The body against my gumboot started to slide so I sat down quickly. Rocks I'd dislodged skittered down the hill.

Help. I'd ride to get help. Find that horseman. This must be the girl's horse. She must be here somewhere. Make her alive and make her safe. Make her alive.

I scrabbled over the rocks up the hill, using roots and broken saplings for handholds. I'd made it to the edge when I heard the noise. It was human but it was almost a bark. A bark of pain.

"Hello? Please? Where are you? Are you okay?"

Stones sliding under my feet. Silence.

Another bark. Along the hillside I could see a brown lump against a tree. It moved. The brown lump had a hand.

"Hello? Are you okay? Hey! Don't move. I'm coming over."

I skidded and bounced against trees until I could see that the lump was a body huddled into an oilskin coat, one leg outstretched, face obscured by a hood.

"Hello? Are you okay? Hello?"

The body shivered. I touched the round of a shoulder and the head shifted. I grabbed the shoulder and shook.

The head snapped back and the air filled with squealing as the girl struggled to get away from me.

"It's okay. Shhhh! I'm not going to hurt you."

She held her chest. "God, you scared the life out of me," she said. She spoke strangely, as if she had a mouthful of chewing gum. Her cheeks were blue with cold. She began to smile weakly and panted.

"Are you okay?" I gasped, laughing with relief. "What happened? Can you walk?"

She touched her ear and shrugged. "I'm hard of hearing," she said. "I can't hear what you're saying. I can't see your lips."

I pulled at the strap on the helmet and only managed to make it tighter so I leaned forward and motioned for her to undo the strap. Her fingers were cold against my neck but nimble. She undid the strap and I ripped the helmet off.

"You're only a boy," she said. "You're a boy!"

I shrugged and felt my face glowing. Yes, I thought, and you're a girl. Not much older than me at a guess. Only a girl.

"Are you okay?" I shouted.

"My ankle," she said. "I think it's busted. Just like in the movies. Stupid girl. Stupid horse. Stupid dead horse."

She bit her lip and tears rolled and hopped across her blue cheeks. She looked away.

She had curly, straw-coloured hair that stuck wet to her neck. Her eyes were a grey blue, like the sky through fog. She smelled like horse and her lips were like Lara Croft's.

"Can you walk?" I shouted.

She sniffed then blew her nose like Wazza had done. Farmer's hankie on to the forest floor.

I tapped her arm and realised it was useless to shout. "Can you walk?"

She shook her head.

"I'll get help," I said.

She shook her head again. "Take me, too. Don't just go . . . take me, too."

"How?"

She held out her hand. "Help me."

I took her cold fingers but she shoved me off and grabbed my thumb in a solid grip. She pulled and groaned and hopped until she was balanced on one good leg.

"Now what?" she asked.

She was shorter than me and built more like a kelpie than a greyhound. I tapped my greyhound hand on my greyhound shoulder. "Piggyback."

"I can't. You can't. I'm too heavy."

"Get on."

I turned and faced up the hill, bending my knees and holding my hands ready.

"I'll squash you."

I tapped my shoulder again. She grabbed my neck and hopped behind me, then counted to three and jumped at two. She made it halfway up my back and I shook her into position. She wasn't as heavy as I thought but she screamed in pain. Right in my ear.

I stooped and grabbed the helmet then began to climb across the slope like a drunken tortoise. The girl screamed in my ear and laughed. Screamed and laughed.

"This is so unreal. I can't believe I did this. I'm so sorry. We're nearly there. Hurry."

I could feel the veins bulging in my temples. Hurry?

"Put me down . . ."

I could see the edge of the track and I knew if I put her down I'd never get her up again. The rock beneath my boots was too crumbly.

"Please. Stop. Put me down. It's . . ."

My greyhound legs were pumping and sliding. My gumboot collected a load of crumbled wet rock. The girl screamed. We slumped on to the track and the girl rolled off and sat there, holding her foot. I huffed and stood up.

"I'm so sorry," she said.

"Don't worry about it. It's okay." I shrugged and sat beside the girl. "Doesn't matter."

"What's your name?" she asked.

"Brad."

"What now, Brad?

"Now you tell me your name is Amber."

Her mouth dropped open.

"And we get out of here," I said and pointed over my shoulder.

She saw the bike and gasped. She slapped my arm. "You hero!"

"What, you reckon I always wear a helmet up the bush?"

"Der," she said and slapped her forehead. "How did you know my name was Amber?"

I touched my nose and helped her to the bike.

I ferried Amber to Merritt's Bridge and stashed the bike. She said she'd wait for her mother or brother to find her but I couldn't leave her. I told her I didn't want to be seen on the bike and she said it was our secret. She talked about how her mum had been driving her crazy and how her brother had been treating her like dirt.

"That sounds like my place, only I have a sister to torture me," I said and she smiled.

"Really?"

Amber told me off a couple of times as we talked. I hadn't realised I was covering my mouth or looking away when I spoke. It didn't take long to get used to the fact that she couldn't hear.

She pulled off her hood and showed me her bionic ear. It was like a toy steering wheel attached beneath her hair and she said she couldn't really hear much better with it, but she could hear herself talk. She told me her email address but I forgot it. She explained that she couldn't use the phone. It took a while, but eventually I started to understand how different the world was for somebody who's hard of hearing.

"Most of the kids at school are fine," she said, "but there are still some idiots who think I'm retarded. They can't cope with anything that's a bit different from what they're used to. Yet they try so hard to be different themselves. They try so hard but they all end up looking the same. The girls are the worst, I reckon. Same hair, same piercings, same make-up."

We looked up and down the road and waited and shivered. I wondered if Huddo and Rick and Wazza had kept the fire going. I offered to give Amber a ride home — her place or mine — but she said she'd rather wait. She didn't really seem to be in a hurry to get back.

We talked until it got dark and she couldn't read my lips. By then I guessed it was around five o'clock and Amber's parents would be totally freaking out. She was shivering hard so I opened my coat and held my arms wide.

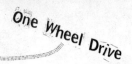

"What are you doing?" she asked.

I stepped closer and she giggled. Then she put her arms around me and I pulled my coat around us both.

I could hear her teeth chattering. She smelled all horsy and wet but I didn't mind. Right then, I liked the smell. She hugged tighter and her cold hands dug under my shirt and came to rest on the skin of my back. I almost squealed but held my breath instead.

She snuggled up even tighter. "Mmm. That's better," she said.

We were together like that for a long time. We didn't speak. Her hands got warm and eventually she stopped shivering. She was resting against me and I was holding her up. My arms were aching but I didn't want to move. I didn't ever want to move. I'd stay there on the bridge all night.

Lights. A car was coming down the road.

Amber jumped and hurt her foot then leaned on the rail of the bridge. I kissed her hand and bolted up the track to where I'd hidden the bike. The car slowed.

"Amber! My baby. Sweetheart. Are you okay? God, you're freezing. Ray? Ray, give us a hand.

She's hurt her leg."

Slamming car doors and the idling engine. I heard Amber's voice as they drove off. She was shouting from the window.

"Thank you! Thank you, my knight in a shiny helmet. Thank you."

I had a secret. After Amber left, I started the bike and lost my night vision as I lit up the bush with the headlight. I rode, slow and steady, back to the campsite.

My pack was there, leaning against a tree, but the boys had gone. The fire was still steaming. They had packed up their wet tents and left before it got too dark.

They would have walked across the bridge. They must have left soon after I rode off on the bike or Amber and I would have met them as they crossed the bridge. In one way, I was glad. I could still sort of feel Amber's hands on my back and I didn't want to disturb that memory. The boys would have trampled all over it. They would have wanted to know every detail but they'd never know. They'd never know unless I told them.

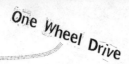

Secret.

Caitlin watched me arrive from the kitchen window. I bumped across the paddock with the light on high beam. Mum still wasn't home from work. The outside lights flicked on and Caitlin stood in her socks on the doorstep.

"What are you doing? That's Dad's bike."

She followed me as I wheeled it into the shed and covered it with the tarp. I'd clean it in the morning. "Yes, I know."

"Mum'll be home any minute. You're dead when I tell her."

"No, don't. I'll tell her and Dad myself."

"When?"

I shrugged. "The first chance I get."

"I'll save you the trouble."

"No."

I could hear the car slowing down on the road. Mum flashed her lights and I waved and slumped my pack against the carport wall. I stepped past Caitlin into the bathroom. I was down to my jocks when Mum knocked. I told her she could come in.

"Get drowned, love?"

"A bit."

"You stink. Did you pee your pants?"

"Might have," I joked. I smelled sweaty. Some of Amber's horsy smell had rubbed off on me, too. "Everything's too wet to tell."

Mum laughed and closed the door.

I knew Caitlin wouldn't tell — she had too many secrets of her own — and I was right. She and Mum made eggs and bacon on toast for dinner and Caitlin looked at me smugly across the table as we ate but I ignored her. Let her unspoken threats just bounce off my shield of happiness.

When Caitlin left to watch TV in her room, Mum and I did the dishes. I almost told her about Amber. Almost blurted it out.

"Did Wazza and Rick go home, too?"

I nodded. "We all looked like drowned poodles."

I phoned and spoke to Wazza later. He wouldn't stop talking and apologising.

"Huddo looked like he was going to start crying," he said. "Rick and I were going to wait for you but we decided we'd walk out with Huddo. It was just too wet and we couldn't keep the fire going. We left your pack up there. Sorry."

"What were you going to do? Carry it home for me?"

"Yeah, well, that's what Rick suggested we should do."

"Did you happen to feel how much the thing weighed?"

Wazza laughed. "I did, actually. That's the main reason we left it behind."

"I picked it up. It's safe in the carport now. I'll deal with it tomorrow."

"Did you find her?"

"Who?"

"The girl. The retard."

"Don't call her that," I snarled. "Don't call anyone that. She's not . . ."

"Whoah. Sorry, Brad. Sorry. The girl. I can't remember her name."

There was a long ugly silence then. Inside, I was wobbling around like I was three years old and someone had stolen one of the training wheels off my bike. I wasn't used to being angry with Wazza. It was a strange feeling. I felt as if I was going to crash. If I had to choose one friend in the world and call him my "best friend", I would have chosen Wazza, without a doubt. But being my best friend didn't give him a free ticket to call people horrible names.

"Amber. Her name's Amber."

"Yeah, sorry." He sounded sheepish. Good.

"I . . . I have to go," I said. "Mum's . . . I have to go."

"Okay," said Wazza suspiciously. "Want to go up the tip again tomorrow, if the weather's okay?"

"Sounds like a plan."

We agreed on a time and I hung up. I slipped my boots on and snuck outside to have a pee on the lemon tree. It had stopped raining for the moment and there were starry holes in the night sky. Until I'd actually met her, helped her, held her, I didn't care who called her what. Something had changed in those few hours we were together.

Caitlin was showered and dressed before nine on Wednesday and she cornered me at the breakfast table.

"You clear out for the day and I promise I won't tell Mum you nicked Dad's bike."

"Blackmail?"

"If you like."

"No deal."

"What?"

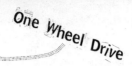

"I'm going with Wazza and Rick up to the tip. I won't be around anyway."

She looked at her hands. "Good."

"I think you should tell Mum."

"What?"

"Not about the bike. About Jordan. If you really love him then you shouldn't have to blackmail me to stay out of your hair or sneak around to see him. Mum's being unfair."

Her face grew red with anger. "You're so full of crap."

I shrugged.

I washed the bike and thought about Amber. I didn't know her home address so I couldn't write. Our computer isn't connected to the Internet so I couldn't have emailed her even if I'd remembered her address. And Amber couldn't use the phone. She might as well be living in Outer Mongolia.

I met Rick and Wazza at the rubbish tip and collected Excalibur from its hiding place in the branch of a tree behind the rubbish pile. Rick found a stack of motorbike magazines and we propped ourselves on a dry car bonnet to read them. Well, look at the pictures. Wazza kept asking me what was wrong.

"Nothing," I said. "Nothing."

"You found her, didn't you?"

"Who?"

"Don't act all innocent. You found Amber."

I nodded.

We flopped into old car seats and I told them. I told them the story straight. Exactly as it had happened. I didn't have to stop to think or retrace my steps and remember what I had already told them, I just told the truth. The story was amazing enough without exaggeration. The horse really had died. Amber really had hurt her foot. I seriously did double her all the way to the bridge.

Amber had told me I was a hero. I didn't have to make that part up. I didn't have to make up anything. I left out the detail of how we hugged each other to keep warm. I didn't mention her horsy smell or how I kissed her hand or what she'd yelled from the car as she left. For one reason or another, I felt awkward about those things.

I couldn't tell them how I was aching to see her again and that, when I hadn't thought about her for ten minutes, and she suddenly popped into

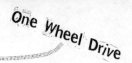

my mind, my guts fluttered the way they did when Mrs Fanshawe asked me to read from a book in front of the whole class.

"My hero," Rick squeaked.

"Shut up," I said, but I couldn't help smiling.

"Gee, you talk rubbish sometimes, Carstairs," said Wazza, punctuating his sentence by smashing a small beer bottle on a lump of concrete.

I felt like going home then. My best friend had called me a liar straight to my face and my body suddenly felt as if it had run out of petrol. Cough, cough. Splutter, splutter. It wouldn't have been so painful if I hadn't been telling the truth for once.

I was about to leave when an old yellow ute turned into the tip road. An old yellow ute with a TV tied proudly on top of a pile of garden waste in the back.

"My TV!" I shouted and the other two cursed. We retreated to the car bodies while the ute was unloaded and I didn't feel like leaving any more.

"You're right," I said to Wazza. "I do spin some rubbish sometimes. Sometimes I exaggerate and tell little white lies. And sometimes I totally make things up."

Wazza shrugged. "Don't we all?"

Rick smiled and nodded his head.

"Just not this time, though. That's exactly what happened. Exactly."

Wazza stared at me for a few seconds. Really looked into my eyes. "Whatever," he finally said.

The ute was leaving. We sprang from our seats and headed for the pile they'd left behind. The TV had been propped against the side of a rusty old water tank. It looked as if it just needed to be switched on.

"Wazza?" I said.

"Hmm?"

I handed him Excalibur. "Would you mind changing the channel for me? The remote doesn't seem to be working."

Wazza grinned. "Serious?"

"It's all yours."

Rick started whining like a five-year-old. "How come Wazza gets to do it? How come I don't get a go? The next television is mine, I don't care who sees it first. That way it's fair and I . . . "

Wazza swung the club above his head and planted the end of it in the dead centre of the tube. It was a lovely shot. The glass collapsed with a healthy whump and crash.

There was a satisfied smile on Wazza's face as he held the club triumphantly above his head, acknowledging the imaginary crowd that was cheering him.

It was probably after one o'clock when we started getting hungry. Rick's not scared to eat food found among the rubbish. One time he found a bag of sherbet cones that were only about three months out of date. They'd never been opened but I still couldn't bring myself to eat one. Neither could Wazza. Rick ate the whole bag by himself with no noticeable side effects.

I have eaten things at the tip, though. When the rubbish pile gets covered with soil, random plants sprout from the garden waste. A pumpkin vine here, a tomato there. Last autumn we found two full-sized watermelons and, honestly, they were better than any I've eaten from the shop. So sweet and fresh.

That's not exactly digging through the rubbish to find food, the way Rick does, but it's certainly eating from the tip. In winter, all the tomatoes are dead and the watermelons are long gone so we decided to cut through the paddocks and forest to Rick and Wazza's place and raid their pantry. Peanut butter sandwiches, it turned out. Wazza wanted to walk to our place and play on the PlayStation but I told him that I'd promised Caitlin that I'd stay away.

"Take us to the dead horse," Rick suggested.

Wazza crossed his arms. "Yeah, come on. Take us to this dead horse."

"Sure," I said and led them along the track and up the hill from the bridge.

"Is it much further?" Rick groaned.

"Nearly there," I said, just as the cutting came into view.

They stood on the edge of the track and swore under their breath at the rounded belly and the single leg pointing at the sky. It was a horrible sight. The rainbow girth strap made it seem nastier, somehow, than if it had been just a wild animal. A dead beetle is nothing. A dead lamb is something else. A dead dog could have been somebody's pet. A dead horse is so big and so dead that it's hard to look at it and the girth strap made it obvious that it had carried a person.

"I believe you," Wazza said, his eyes wide.

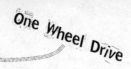
One Wheel Drive

"Let's go down," Rick suggested.

"No," Wazza and I chorused.

"We should be getting back," Wazza said. "It'll be dark soon."

Rick didn't need any more encouragement to leave.

Caitlin found some lamb chops in the freezer and made a full meal. Mashed potatoes, peas, mint jelly, everything. She put it on the table as Mum pulled into the drive.

Another car parked behind her. An old white ute dusted with red.

Caitlin ran out in her socks. Dad had grown a beard, a bushy grey and black thing that sparkled with tears. His face was tanned and more wrinkled than I remembered.

"Too long," he groaned.

We howled and hugged. All of us. I hid my face against Dad's chest and made my own private sniffling wet patch on his shirt.

It was a special occasion. I was allowed to cry.

It started raining but we didn't move. Dad sighed and squeezed us tighter.

After that delicious meal (reheated in the microwave), we sat in the lounge and unloaded our secrets.

Mum said she had wanted to kill Caitlin.

Dad stroked his beard.

"I feel like that was my fault," I said. "Caitlin pushed me and I stumbled into the door frame. Mum didn't hear the whole story. She thought Caitlin punched me. Sorry."

Mum apologised to Caitlin again and hugged her around the head. Caitlin apologised to Mum and me for being so horrible to live with. She said she was in love with Jordan and started crying again. She said she loved him and that it wasn't fair that they weren't allowed to see each other.

I bit my lip. My sister should go for a career in acting or politics, I thought.

They talked about her and the party where she got wasted and Caitlin was saying sorry again.

Dad kept rubbing his temples like it was all a bit much but they kept talking. Caitlin went on and on about Jordan and Mum offered to drop her in town on her way to work in the morning so she could spend the day with him, if it was okay with his parents. Caitlin sprang into the kitchen to phone him. I was beginning to understand her excitement.

"I nicked Dad's bike," I said.

Mum and Dad stared, open-mouthed.

"I started riding it in the paddocks, then I took it into the reserve. I came back along the Brandy Creek Road and I got pulled over by the police."

Dad looked at Mum and they sighed.

"What happened?" Dad asked.

I shrugged. "Nothing. He told me off. Told me not to ride on the roads. Said he'd book me if he saw me again. He said he knows you and said to say hello but I didn't catch his name. I thought I was going to jail, for sure."

"Probably David Rich," Dad said and shook his head. "You obviously didn't hurt yourself . . . Is the bike okay?"

"Yes. I cleaned it and put it back in the shed."

"And told us about it anyway," he said.

I nodded. "Oh and I owe you a new visor for your helmet. It got caught on a branch."

Dad stroked his beard again and huffed at Mum. "I don't know. I go off to work, I come home again and my family have gone wild."

I wanted to tell them about Amber. How I'd

found her. How I'd doubled her to the bridge with her foot hanging out the side and how she'd moaned and complained into the back of the helmet. I wanted to tell that story as straight as I'd told Wazza and Rick but Caitlin came bubbling back in to say that Jordan's parents were fine with her spending the day at their place tomorrow.

Dad had a confession of his own. He'd needed his account number the other day so he could be paid. The manager sold a tractor before the station went bust and sent the money to the men who were owed wages. Dad got nine thousand dollars. The manager told Dad that he couldn't sleep at night thinking there was an angry mob of shearers after his neck.

We were more like a family that night than I ever remembered. It wasn't all smiles, though. Dad still didn't have a job. The nine thousand would stop us from going under, but not forever. Caitlin would still rather live in town. Mum would rather not go to the job she hated.

The phone rang at eleven. Late for a phone call. It was one of Dad's shearing mates. I crawled into bed and felt as if I was floating. All the pressure had gone. It was like I'd been to the tip and emptied all the rubbish out of my life. And maybe found some treasure. Dad came to sit on the bed later and woke me up.

"Don't ride on the roads. It's dangerous on the bush tracks but on the roads you could run into something or someone else and there's no insurance to cover you for that."

I wriggled back under the covers and nodded.

"I was disappointed you took my bike. Shocked, really. You've always been such a responsible kid. And then I got disappointed in myself for not being around to make sure you did it safely. Properly. Sounds like you handled yourself okay. . . "

I blinked and looked at him. I hadn't gone into that much detail.

Dad stared stony-faced for a minute, then smiled.

"That was Jacko on the phone. He said that while he was on his way back from Queensland his daughter went off the rails and nicked his horse."

I sat up.

"Sounds like she got into a bit of trouble. The horse slipped off the bank. She was lucky. She got a badly bruised ankle. The horse died."

I swallowed, my stomach doing the flutter-

flutter thing again.

"They're coming out tomorrow. For some strange reason, the daughter reckons you might know where the dead horse is."

I nodded.

Dad chuckled and rubbed his eyes. "They're coming to collect the saddle and pay their last respects."

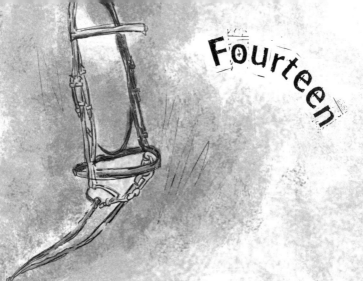

They arrived in a mud-caked twin-cab ute. Jacko was a big bloke, not wiry like my father but big and hairy, as if he would benefit from being on the other side of the shears for a change. He shook my hand and I felt like a kindergarten kid beside him. He had a big hairy laugh to match his big hairy body.

I saw Amber in the passenger seat of the car and my whole body blushed. My brain stalled and I couldn't even manage a hello. I couldn't look at her. She was beautiful. She was so beautiful that if I looked at her I knew I'd stare and make an idiot out of myself.

Amber hopped out of the car and adjusted her jeans. Her left foot was bandaged. The toes that stuck out the end were blue. She looked into the paddock then hopped and sat on the bull bar of

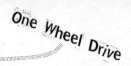

their ute, her work boot tucked behind the bottom rail and sore foot swinging free. Her dad slapped the bonnet twice and she turned.

"This is Leigh. I think you've met Bradley."

Amber blushed, too, and said hi.

Jacko asked if I could show him where the horse was and I told him I could.

"Can we get the ute in there?" he asked.

I shrugged. "Can get close."

Dad offered Jacko a beer but the big bloke said he'd like to get to the horse first.

"You jump in the front, Brad. Give us directions. Coming for the ride?" he asked Dad.

"Yeah. I want to hear the story."

"Hop in the back with Amber the storyteller."

Amber told Dad how she'd got angry with her mum and run away from home on Jemma. How she'd got lost. How the horse had slipped in the wet and fallen down the hillside. How it happened so fast that she didn't know what was going on and how horrible it was to find the dead horse when she finally came to her senses. How she was convinced that she was going to die, too.

She said I'd scared her when I found her and helped her get back to the bridge. She skilfully avoided any reference to the motorbike.

"I nicked my dad's motorbike," I told Jacko. "I doubled her to the bridge."

Jacko looked across at me with one eyebrow raised. He and Dad started laughing.

"What did he say?" Amber asked.

"He said he nicked my motorbike and doubled you to the bridge," Dad shouted.

"You don't need to shout, Dad. She can read your lips."

We crossed Merritt's Bridge and Jacko slipped it into four-wheel drive. The ute bucked over the ruts and I held the handrail above the glove box.

"How much further?" Jacko asked.

"Not far. Five Ks maybe."

"Is there anywhere to turn around?

"I don't know," I said. There would have been plenty of room to turn a bike around but the track didn't seem as bumpy in one-wheel drive either.

Jacko drove right to the cutting that had fallen across the road. Right to the spot where I'd parked the bike.

"Now what?" he asked.

"This is it," Amber said. "I remember all those rocks. Jemma's down the side of the hill."

Jacko did a fifteen-point turn and parked facing the way we'd come in. He and Dad popped their doors and got out.

"You want a lift?" he asked Amber.

She shook her head. "I'll wait in the car."

I said I'd wait with her and Jacko smiled. He and Dad gently picked their way over the edge of the cliff. I grabbed the headrest and faced the girl in the seat behind me.

"How's your foot?"

"Much better. Only hurts if I bump it now."

Her chin crinkled and she wiped at her eyes.

I touched her knee and she grabbed my hand and pulled it to her cheek.

"Sorry, Brad. Sorry for getting you into all this. Sorry for telling."

I shrugged. "I wanted to see you again. It was a great excuse. Thanks. I'd already told my dad that I nicked his bike."

She sniffed and let go of my hand then dug a hankie from her pocket to blow her nose.

Dad popped up from the cliff and dropped a bridle into the back of the ute. It clattered, metal on metal, and Amber turned to look through the window.

I touched her knee. "Did you hear that?"

"No. Felt it."

"Are they going to drag her up with the ute?" I asked.

"No. I don't think so."

"Bury her?"

She shook her head. "It was a good place to die. She can go back to the earth here. Rest in peace, hey?"

She seemed so calm about it all. I realised the dead horse for her was like a dead lamb for me. It was sad but not always crying sad. You just do what you can. You can't bury a horse halfway down a cliff. Amber wasn't being mean, she was being practical. She popped her door and swung her legs out.

"What are you doing?"

"I . . . I want to see her again. Say goodbye."

I got out and backed up to her door to piggy-back her.

She smiled and grabbed my shoulders. "You're a brave boy, Brad. Very brave."

I carried her to the edge of the track and she rested her chin on my shoulder. The men had dug the saddle free and were carrying it solemnly up the hill. Jacko lowered it into the ute and turned, grave-faced, back down the hill. He and Dad broke branches from the dogwoods and laid them over the horse until the shape had disappeared. You wouldn't have known it was there if you weren't looking for it. They had buried it, in a way, and in a few months it would return to the earth like Amber said.

It was quiet in the ute on the way back home. Dad was in the front with the window cranked right down, looking at everything, breathing the cool air and sighing. Amber held my hand. She kept squeezing my fingers and smiling. I squeezed her fingers back. She dropped my hand as we pulled into our driveway and when the car stopped she opened her door and grinned at me.

"Hurry up, slave," she said. "Chop chop. I need a lift. Aren't you going to show me around?"

Dad and Jacko went inside for a beer and I piggybacked Amber around the yard.

"Ah, so this is your machinery shed," she said. "And this is your woodpile. This is all very exciting, slave, but I need to go to the toilet."

I carted her around to the back door and almost dropped her while I was trying to kick my boots off. She squealed right in my ear and didn't know she was doing it. She groaned as we bumped into the wall and I lowered her gently on to her good foot at the bathroom door.

"Thank you, slave," she said. "That will be all for now. I'll summon you if I need you again."

Dad and Jacko had beers and were settled in the lounge. The TV was on but muted. I poured a Coke for Amber and one for myself. The whole house shook as she hopped into the lounge from the bathroom.

"Like an elephant on a pogo stick," Jacko said.

"Shut up!" Amber bawled and slapped her dad on the arm. She lowered herself on to the couch and I gave her the drink.

"Thank you, slave. That will be all," she said and waved me away with the back of her hand.

Jacko stomped his foot on the floor. "Be nice," he mouthed.

"I was joking," she said aloud. "Brad knew I was joking, didn't you, Brad?"

I smiled. I could think of worse things than being her slave and it *had* felt like a joke.

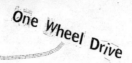

Amber was watching the newsreader on the muted TV.

"See that, Dad? Train crash in Adelaide."

She had watched the newsreader's lips and followed the whole story without hearing a thing.

I touched her knee and pointed to the TV. "That's amazing," I said.

"What? Train crash?"

"No, that you can lip-read the TV."

"Is the sound off?"

I nodded.

She shrugged. "Do you have a chess set?"

I nodded again.

"Want a game?"

"Don't," said Jacko sternly. "You don't want to play chess with her. She cheats."

"I do not," Amber complained. "You just can't handle being beaten by your own daughter. He's a sore loser."

We set up the chessboard and in ten minutes I'd lost my queen. Three moves later, it was checkmate. She was good and she showed no mercy.

Jacko had finished his beer and refused another when Dad offered.

He waved to Amber. "Come on, hop-along," he

said. "We'd better get going."

"But I'm just warming up," she said, flexing her fingers.

"Maybe Brad can come over some time?"

"That's a good idea," Dad said.

Jacko explained where they lived as he piggy-backed Amber out to the car. I realised I'd been past their place about a million times — on the bus, in the car, on my bike. They lived a kilometre or so from Turnbull Reserve. The Jacksons lived — surprise, surprise — on Jackson's Track. Dad knew all this, apparently, just hadn't bothered to mention it. Not that I'd asked or anything.

Amber didn't live in Outer Mongolia after all. Just a short bike ride from home. Their place was closer to home than the tip.

I rode my bike to Rick and Wazza's house that afternoon and found the boys building a sled to tow behind their four-wheeled motorbike. They'd built a timber frame and lined it with flat steel cut from a shop sign they'd salvaged. It had a rope handle nailed to the front and the plastic seat part from an old school chair screwed to the top. When

I arrived, they were trying to attach the tow-rope to the frame.

"Where you been?" Rick asked.

"Home," I said. "Amber and her dad came over and I showed them where the horse was so they could collect the saddle and that."

"Did they bury it?" Wazza asked.

"Sort of. Covered it with branches."

"How's your girlfriend?" Rick teased.

I shrugged and smiled. "She's okay."

"Whoohoo," Rick said. "Brad's in love."

"Don't know about that," I said. "Amber's a girl and she's my friend. She's cool. Beat me at chess this morning — good and proper. It was embarrassing."

Rick and Wazza both laughed without pity and that was all we said about Amber. I thought about her a few times that afternoon. She just popped into my head but my tummy didn't tingle.

I knew I'd go and visit her before the end of the holidays but that afternoon I was busy. Busy getting minor spinal injuries and laughing my head off. We took it in turns wearing Wazza's bike helmet and bumping around on the sled and they let me drive the four-wheeler for the first time. I got to give Wazza a bit of whiplash and roll him out on a hard corner. The four-wheeler was fun but not as much fun as the two-wheeler.

We found a little mound of dirt and Wazza dragged Rick over it fast enough for the sled to get airborne. He hit the ground hard and rolled off but, when I ran over to inspect his wounds, he was laughing. So we did it again. And again. And again. There wasn't much blood lost. We each collected a few bruises but we hardly got hurt at all. Bit surprising, really.

Fifteen

It was the middle Sunday of the holidays when I rode my bike along Jackson's Track to Amber's place. A border collie strained at its chain and barked wildly at me but its tail was spinning flat out like an electric fan. My heart was beating harder than it should have and my guts were doing that mad tingle thing again.

Jacko appeared from the machinery shed to see what the dog was barking about. His hands and forearms were greasy-grubby black and he held some sort of engine part.

"Dog!" he growled and the collie stopped barking. "It's only young Mr Carstairs. How are you, Brad?"

"Good thanks, Jacko . . . Mr Jackson."

"Jacko's fine," he said.

"What are you working on?"

"Just giving the Fergy a bit of love and kindness. Grease and oil mostly."

He nodded at the old grey tractor parked in the first bay.

"Amber's inside. I think she'll be glad to see you. Her ankle's getting better but she's going out of her mind with boredom. Just go in the back door."

"Thanks," I said and leaned my bike against the wire fence. I followed a path to the back door and kicked my boots on top of the mixed pile of shoes beside the path.

"Brad?" Jacko shouted.

"Yes?"

"Take your boots off, mate, or Mrs Jacko will kill us both."

"Okay," I yelled and smiled to myself. I was smiling, but my heart was still banging away in my chest like I'd ridden my bike from Mt Everest, not Brandy Creek Road.

The house was quiet. I slipped through the back door into the laundry, banged the door shut and walked heavily into the kitchen.

I found Amber lying on the couch in the lounge. She had her feet propped on the armrest at one

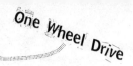

end and her face buried in a book.

I coughed into my hand but she didn't move. I stomped my foot on the floorboards and she looked up. She'd been munching an apple and she almost choked when she realised it was me.

"Oh, my goodness," she yelled. "Brad! What are you doing here?"

"Came to see how you were going."

"Oh, my goodness," she said again, blushing a deep red. She swung her feet carefully to the floor and tried to hide behind her hair.

I waited until she was looking at me again. At least she was smiling now.

"I can go," I said. "If you want to keep reading."

"Don't be stupid!"

She was struggling to stand so I moved to help her but she playfully slapped me away.

"Let's get out of here," she said, limping heavily to the back door.

Her bruised ankle wasn't bandaged any more and she carefully threaded it into a gumboot. She waved her hand at me impatiently as she limped off up the path. "Chop chop."

By the time I'd slipped on my boots and caught up with her she had stumped out to the machinery shed and was watching her father working on the tractor.

She raised one finger. "Guided tour," she said. "This is my dad, Jacko. You can tell by all the hair that he's part ape. We haven't worked out yet which part it is but Mum thinks it's his brain."

Jacko looked up from the tractor, his teeth bared in a comical snarl.

"Be careful," she said. "He bites. And this is our grey Ferguson tractor that some bright spark named Fergy. That's my brother's motorbike that he doesn't ride any more. And over here is our dog that some bright spark named Dog."

I tapped her shoulder. "You have a dog named Dog?"

"Yes. Stupid, I know. It was the great ape's idea. Apparently it's from a cartoon."

She showed me their chickens, their stockyard, her brother's horse. I recognised the horse: it was the one the man had ridden into our campsite.

"How old is your brother?"

"Ray? Nineteen."

"He came looking for you on that horse," I said. "He rode through our camp. I thought he was your dad."

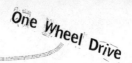

"No way," she snorted. "Sometimes he bosses me around and likes to think he's my dad but I just ignore him."

The horse's name was Stalin and we climbed the rails on the yard to pat him. He nuzzled Amber and sniffed at me before trotting to the other side of the paddock.

Amber sat on the top rail, her elbows on her knees, chin in her hands and sighed. "The holidays are so boring."

"You must be joking."

She shook her head. "Why? What have you been doing?"

I shrugged. "Riding with my friends. Trying to go camping in the rain. Towing each other around on a sled behind the four-wheeler."

"Saving damsels in distress."

I laughed then and felt my cheeks get hot. "We've been up the tip."

"The rubbish tip? Wow, that must have been exciting," she said sarcastically.

"It is!" I said and pushed her knee. "We smash stuff, blow up old aerosol cans and find some amazing things."

"Yeah?"

"You should come and see for yourself."

"Anything would be better than lying around here all day."

"Okay, tomorrow."

Amber screwed up her face. "My ankle still hurts too much to walk all that way."

"I could double you."

"On your dad's motorbike?"

"No, my pushbike."

"The extra weight will kill you."

"I double Wazza and Rick all the time and they're both heavier than you."

She looked at me with a lopsided grin.

"Tomorrow," I said. "Pick you up round ten."

She shrugged one shoulder. "Okay."

We were quiet then for a full minute. Thoughts tumbled around in my head. How would Amber go meeting Wazza and Rick? Or, more to the point, how would Wazza and Rick treat Amber? Would they laugh at the way she speaks? Would they be rude? Would they talk to each other at all?

"You want a game of chess?" she asked.

I said I would but Amber had a smile on her face that made me think it was my first dumb move for the day. It was like I was a lamb and the fox had just asked me if I'd like to go for a walk. Of course!

We played and, predictably, I lost. She made us ham, cheese and tomato toasted sandwiches and chocolate milkshakes with extra ice cream.

The more time I spent with her, the funnier she got. She wasn't just a little bit smart, she was brilliant. She wasn't accidentally good at chess, she was a wizard and the more I looked at her and laughed with her, the stranger our first meeting seemed. It was as if the girl I had found with the dead horse was a different person from the one who thrashed me so convincingly at chess.

Maybe I was a different person, too. I'd held her and kept her warm on the bridge. I'd even kissed her hand. And the more time we spent together, the weirder that seemed. I liked her a lot but I didn't think it was the same way Jordan liked Caitlin. Sending her a love note would feel like sending a love note to Wazza and that would be totally weird. She wasn't my girlfriend. She was just my friend.

The score was six-nil when I realised it was

getting late. I took her queen in the last game and, for a few moves, I seemed to be winning. But she still managed to pin my king with a lowly knight and a bishop.

She hobbled along beside me to my bike.

"Take me out to the mailbox?" she asked.

I moved forward and let her climb on to the seat. She held my hips and I stood on the pedals as we wobbled across the drive and past the machinery shed. The shed lights were on.

"See you, Jacko," I yelled.

"Oh, right-oh, Brad," Jacko said. "Thanks for coming over. See you soon."

Amber was a good passenger. She wasn't all shaky and clingy like Wazza, she just seemed to enjoy the ride. I stopped beside the milk-can letterbox on the side of Jackson's Track and she stepped off carefully. It was Sunday. There was never going to be any mail but she looked in the can anyway.

I felt awkward. I didn't know how to say good-bye. If it was Rick or Wazza or Huddo that I was leaving, I'd pedal off and wave over my shoulder, but it was Amber.

"Thanks for coming over," she said.

"Thanks for having me."

She nodded and gave a little wave, then began stumping her way back to the house.

I watched her over my shoulder as I started towards home. She turned and waved again, this time with two hands above her head. I gave her a big wave back and pedalled home with a smile on my face.

Caitlin had been much easier to live with since she'd been spending her days in town with Jordan and her other friends. She'd changed. She smiled randomly when we were in each other's company (which was way out of character) and brought home a DVD she thought I might like.

"It came with a motorbike magazine Jordan bought and he was going to throw it out. I thought you might like it." (So totally out of character that I was stunned.)

"What do you say?" Mum said.

"Pardon?"

"What do you say to your sister?"

"Oh, thanks, Caitlin. Thanks heaps." I leaned in and kissed her cheek.

She wiped her face with her hand then wiped the hand on my shirt. "All right, all right. No need

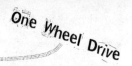

to get carried away."

I put the DVD on while Mum and Caitlin were doing the dishes. They talked all the time now, Mum and Caitlin. It was like the girls hung out together and the boys hung out together.

The DVD was awesome — Crusty Demons, Metal Mulisha. They were doing massive jumps and stunts and Dad put down his paper to watch it with me.

"Unbelievable," he said.

I had to agree.

The phone rang and Caitlin answered it. She was chatting away for five minutes as if it was one of her friends she was talking to.

"It's an art form, isn't it?" Dad said.

"You think?"

"Oh, absolutely. When it's in slow motion like that, it's motorised ballet."

"Ballet where they regularly break bones and people have died."

Dad laughed.

"Brad, phone," Caitlin said.

Dad paused the movie.

"It's Wazza," she said and gave me the handset.

She'd been talking to Wazza? She'd been talking

to one of my friends for five minutes?

"Waz?"

"What's got into your sister? She was being all civilised all of a sudden. I actually had a conversation with her. I haven't had a conversation with her since we were in primary school. Thought she hated my guts."

"Tell me about it," I said. I held the mouthpiece close and whispered. "I think an alien might have taken over her body."

Wazza laughed and we arranged to meet at the tip the following day. I didn't mention Amber. I could have. Maybe I should have — it might have calmed the butterflies in my stomach — but I didn't.

I slept okay. The activity in my stomach didn't start again until after I left the Jacksons' place with my passenger on the back.

It's hard when your friends meet for the first time, I discovered. I wanted it all to go smoothly and I wanted everybody to get along but I had my doubts.

I couldn't talk to Amber while she was sitting

behind me on my bike — she couldn't see my lips. I wanted to tell her about Wazza and Rick. I wanted to tell her that they can be pretty rough at times and, if they said something stupid, not to worry about it because they would probably be joking and . . .

"Who's that?" Amber said. She was pointing to two forms climbing over the fence on the side of the road just ahead of us.

Rick and Wazza.

I hadn't warned her. I hadn't had a chance to tell her anything.

We rolled to a stop beside them. They were smiling like idiots.

"Hello!" Rick shouted and waved to Amber. It was a funny sort of cartoon wave and Wazza did the same. I wanted to hide. This was a bad idea.

"Hi," said Amber. "You're the Turnbull boys, aren't you?"

Rick and Wazza looked at each other, stunned.

"Your mum and my mum work together," she said. "I sometimes see you in your car. Red Mitsubishi four-wheel drive."

"That's right," Wazza shouted and held out his hand. "I'm Warren."

Amber shook his paw. "You don't have to yell," she said. "I can read your lips when you're looking at me."

Wazza blushed. "Sorry."

Rick was next in line for a handshake. He formed his name carefully on his lips and resisted the urge to shout.

She took his fingers. "Hi, Rick. I'm Amber."

"We … were … just … going … up … to … the … rubbish . . . tip," Wazza said. He was still speaking loudly. "Do . . . you . . . want . . . to . . . come?"

"We'll race you," Amber said and slapped my backside. "Giddy up, Brad. Go, come on!"

I yelped and pedalled like crazy. We had to ride up the track while Rick and Wazza cut through the paddock. We still beat them, just.

Amber was crowing like a rooster and punching her fists in the air.

"You had a head start," Rick whinged, but he was smiling.

Amber patted my head. "Well done, Brad. Good boy. You ran a great race. I wish I had an apple to give you."

I neighed and Amber stepped off the bike on to her good leg. Her first few paces looked painful but she didn't make a sound. She held her nose.

"You didn't tell me that it smelled so good," she said.

"You ... get ... used ... to ... it," Wazza yelled.

Amber followed Rick over to the line of new rubbish.

"Just talk normal," I said to Wazza. "Make sure she can see your lips and talk normally."

"Sorry," he said. "I'm just not used to ..."

There was the sound of breaking glass. Amber had smashed a wine bottle with a lump of wood.

Rick swore and jumped back in fright.

Amber held her makeshift club aloft, a crazy grin on her face.

Rick was running from her in mock horror.

Amber hobbled after him for a couple of steps, screaming a battle cry, then lowered her club to the rubbish and began poking through the bags at her feet.

"Fifty cents!" she cried. "I'm rich!"

I walked over and tapped Amber's shoulder. "The rules are that we share anything we find at the tip. Including money. I think it's my turn to hold the coin."

She pushed me away with a smile. "Get off, you

numbskull. I found it, I'm keeping it."

Rick found an empty can of spray paint. The little marble thing inside it still rattled but no spray came out when he pressed the nozzle. He shook it and did a little dance, shaking it as if it was a musical instrument.

Wazza found an active chimney. It was so hot that no smoke was making it to the surface — so hot that it was hard to look into. The sides glowed with embers.

"What is it?" Amber asked. "A volcano?"

"Just a fire," Wazza said, talking normally now. "It burns in the rubbish underground."

"Cool," Amber said.

Rick held his spray can over the fiery hole for a second then let it drop. He bumped into me in his hurry to get away.

Amber just stood there and watched.

I grabbed her sleeve and tried to drag her clear. She shook me off. "I want to watch."

"It's going to explode," I said and grabbed her arm. "Come on!"

She reluctantly hobbled away with me. We'd almost made it to the safety of the car bodies when the can went off. It was a good bang and we turned

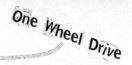

to see coals and burned rubbish showering down around the hole.

"Whoah!" Amber said. "Excellent!"

"Could you hear that?" Rick asked her, but she wasn't looking at him.

I shook her sleeve and pointed to Rick. He repeated the question.

"No. Felt it," she said. She put her hand over her stomach and made an explosion sound with her mouth.

The guys laughed.

"What can you hear?" Rick asked.

"Nothing much," she said.

"Doesn't that hearing aid thing work?" he said, touching his ear.

"Rick!" I grumbled and scowled at him. I wanted to tell him to shut up. Just leave her alone. She is how she is. Just accept that. I wanted to say all those things but another part of me wanted to know. They were things I wanted to know more about but was too scared to ask.

"It works," she said. "Mostly I hear a little bit of my own voice. It makes it easier to speak if you can hear yourself speak. Even a tiny bit."

The boys were nodding now.

"Can you do sign language?" Wazza asked and moved his hands.

"A little," she said.

Rick waved. "What does this mean?"

"Um, it means 'hello'?"

"No, not that. This," he said and touched his brow with one finger. He tucked his hands under his arms and strutted around like a chicken before patting his backside with both hands.

"Um, does it mean, 'I feel like an egg for breakfast'?"

"No, it means, 'Your brains are made of chicken poop'."

"It does not," Wazza groaned.

"No, it does. Pete Quentin told me."

Wazza and I moaned together. Pete Quentin was the biggest fool in the southern hemisphere. Second biggest fool, it seemed.

"Can you teach us sign language?" Wazza asked.

"Not really. I've had my bionic ear since I was four. Some people learn how to lip-read and talk. Some people learn how to sign. Some do a bit of both. Mostly, I talk. Don't I, Brad?"

I smiled and nodded.

"Sometimes," she said, "you can't shut me up."

But she did shut up then and so did Rick and Wazza. There was a big awkward hole in the conversation and my stomach started doing its flutter thing.

I knew it wouldn't work out, these friends meeting. It was a silly thing to do, bringing Amber to the tip. Now everyone was feeling really strange and . . .

"Well," Amber said. "That explosion was awesome. Can we do it again?"

Rick grinned and trotted back to the rubbish pile. I collected Excalibur.

When I met up with them again, they'd found four more cans: toilet spray, furniture polish and two dead pressure packs of fly spray.

"Ho!" Wazza said, as he struggled to pull something from beneath a pile of rubble. "I've struck gold!"

He'd dragged his find clear by the time we'd negotiated the rough ground to him. It was a gas bottle. A rusty old cylinder that had once powered somebody's barbecue or camping stove. He shook it and held it close to his ear.

"Feels like it's still got gas in it," he said, twisting the tap on top of the cylinder. It hissed. His eyes grew wide and he began picking his way towards the chimney.

If anything, the hole seemed to be glowing hotter since Rick's paint can had opened it up.

"Are you going to chuck that in?" Rick asked his brother.

"I don't know. Could be a bit risky."

"Come on," Rick urged. "There's nobody except us here. It will go off!"

We had an empty aerosol can each and Rick had his hanging over the hole in the ground.

"Ready?"

"Not yet," Wazza said. "Let's do them together."

"Okay," Amber said, setting herself up beside Rick. Wazza and I did the same.

"Somebody has to count," Amber said.

"On three," Rick said. "One . . . two . . . three!"

We dropped our cans and three of us scattered. Wazza grabbed the gas cylinder with both hands.

"What the heck," he cried. "Fire in the hole! Run for it!"

I looked over my shoulder to see him plunge the gas bottle into the flames.

"Excalibur!" I yelled. I'd put it down beside the hole. When the gas bottle went up, it would destroy my trusty club for sure. It's hard to explain how attached you can get to a bent old golf stick. I bet golfers have special clubs, too, I thought. I had to get it.

I knew I still had a few seconds — maybe even a minute — until the bombs started to explode, so I ran back to get Excalibur.

"Brad?" Amber yelled. "What are you doing? Get away!"

I had the club by then and I'd turned to bolt to safety when the ground under my feet gave way. It opened like a trapdoor beneath me and suddenly I was waist-deep in the rubbish. Ash and heat surged around me and filled my lungs. I'd fallen into a burning hole less than three metres from the chimney where Wazza had thrown the gas bottle. My feet couldn't find anything to stand on. Everything that felt like a step disintegrated. I was kicking at nothing.

"Brad!" Amber screamed.

Rick and Wazza had made it to the safety of the car bodies but Amber had only limped half the way.

I was screaming then. The more I kicked and struggled, the more the burning rubbish around me crumbled. The dragon was swallowing me.

Hot coals were biting through my jeans and some had fallen into my boot and were burning the top of my foot. There was a moment — what felt like a very long moment — when I really did think I was about to die.

But help arrived. It arrived in the form of Amber. She grabbed my jacket and heaved. The fabric started to rip and I couldn't believe how strong she was. She was shaking and making noises like a professional weightlifter and suddenly I was above the ground again and scrambling away with her beside me.

The gas bottle exploded like a bomb, setting up a shockwave that knocked us flat on to the rubbish. We covered our heads as a flash of heat followed that felt hotter than the sun. I held my breath as bits of rubbish and embers fell around us.

Smaller blasts followed — probably the aerosols — but I didn't come out from under my arms.

When the ash and mess stopped drumming on my back and the explosions stopped, when the battle was finally over and I slowly uncovered my head, my ears were ringing. Wazza's hand was on my shoulder, his face creased with panic.

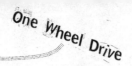

"Are you okay?"

I nodded and sat up. Something was burning in my boot. I kicked it off and shook a coal from the top of my sock.

Amber wasn't moving.

Rick was gently shaking her shoulder. "Amber?"

I grabbed her arm and she unfolded like a turtle that had realised that the coast was finally clear. The boys sighed with relief as she sat up.

"Are you okay, Brad?" she asked.

I nodded. "You?"

She dusted herself down. There was no blood. No damage done. She was smiling then. Literally grinning from ear to ear.

"How unbelievably awesome was that?" she said. "I *heard* that one!"

"I think they heard that one in Gellerton," Wazza said. He wasn't smiling. "We'd better go before someone comes looking."

Amber limped to the place where the gas bottle had blown up. "Whoah! Check it out."

The explosion had torn a crater in the rubbish that was about three metres across. Wedged into one wall were the blackened remains of the cylinder. The steel had torn apart like paper.

"Should have seen the fireball," Rick said. "It was higher than the trees. Ten metres, maybe more."

Wazza was retreating from the mess, looking pale. "You were lucky you weren't killed," he said. "There were bits of metal flying off that could have cut you to pieces."

"Shrapnel," Rick said.

"Exactly," said his brother. "Sorry, you guys. That was stupid."

Amber had been watching him. "It's okay, Warren. We're fine. We're all fine."

Wazza nodded and just kept walking.

"Waz, wait up," said Rick, jogging after him.

I collected my bike and took Amber home in silence. The ringing in my ears had gone by the time I parked beside the Jacksons' machinery shed.

Amber was still smiling. "Thanks, Brad," she said as she carefully stepped off the bike. "Coming in for a drink?"

I shook my head. I wanted to go home.

"Thanks," I said.

"What for?"

"For coming back for me."

She laughed and snorted at the same time. "That's okay. You would have done it for me.

We're even now, hey?"

"But . . ."

She held up a single finger to silence me. "That's what friends do."

I nodded and looked at my hands.

"Besides," she said. "I had fun. Probably more fun than a girl should, blowing things up at the tip, but I can't help that. I am who I am. I like what I like." And she play-punched my arm.

I couldn't help smiling then. I liked what I liked, too, and Amber was certainly one of those things. I liked how everything was a competition for her. I liked her loud mouth and her stupid, sarcastic sense of humour. I liked her tomboy's sense of adventure.

We find friends in the strangest places.

Wazza phoned that night. He said it was just for a chat but I think he wanted to make sure Amber and I were okay. And to apologise once more.

"I won't be doing that again in a hurry," he said.

"Come on, Wazza. We're fine. You know what they say — all the good stunts are accidents to begin with."

Sixteen

He laughed. "Yeah, I guess so. We'll be going back to school next week for a rest."

"Exactly! That's how the holidays should be."

"Too right."

The ute wasn't in the carport when I got up on Thursday morning. It wasn't late but Mum and Dad had both gone out. Mum would have gone to work and maybe taken Caitlin into town. I didn't know where Dad was. He hadn't left a note.

I checked the sheep. Two more lambs had been born overnight. They looked happy and healthy enough, wobbling around like they were on stilts and bleating their pathetic little baas until their mothers found them. Everything felt new and alive and I realised I could smell springtime, even though it was still more than a month until the calendar said it was spring. The air was sweet and clean and I could feel the morning sun warming the backs of my hands.

I saw Dad's ute coming along Brandy Creek Road and started towards the house. At least I thought it was Dad's ute. It had the old green canvas tarp over something in the back.

Dad was in the shed when I made it home. He had a big grin on his face. "Morning, Brad."

"What?" I asked suspiciously.

"What what?"

"Why are you smiling?"

"No reason," he said and looked away.

"What's in the ute?"

"Ute? Which ute? Oh, my ute? Nothing."

I walked over to the carport and Dad appeared beside me, still smiling. He grabbed the corner of the tarp and looked me in the eyes. "Bit of an early birthday present for you," he said and yanked the cover aside.

It was a motorbike. An XR. It was dusty and the stickers had been rubbed blank in a few spots, but it looked like heaven to me.

"Needs a bit of work but it runs okay. It's nothing special but it was the right price, if you know what I mean."

Nothing special, he says. It was a miracle. It was better than a miracle and I spent some more of the tears I'd saved for special occasions. I hugged my dad and sobbed into his chest. He laughed quietly

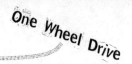

and stroked my head then I was on the back of
the ute, dusting the machine with my hand and
wiping my eyes on my sleeve.

"What do you think?" Dad said.

I thought I was going to explode. I thought I
was going to burst right then and there and I did,
in a way. I jumped up and down and punched the
air over my head and crowed like a rooster.

"There are going to be some rules," said Dad,
all serious, but still with a smile on his face.

"Yes, Dad."

"No going off the farm."

I stuck my bottom lip out.

"I'm serious," he said.

"Yes, Dad. No going off the farm."

"And always wear a helmet."

"Will my bike helmet be okay? Could I use
your helmet, the full-face one?"

Dad opened the ute door and grabbed a shiny
MX helmet with stickers all over it. "Here," he
said, tossing it to me. "See if that fits."

There were cobwebs inside and I dusted them
clear and slipped it on. It fitted as if it had been
made for my head. It was so light and comfortable
and I could do up the strap with one hand. I

jiggled on the spot and spun around with my arms wide.

We cleaned the bike up together and checked it over, adjusted the brakes, changed the oil and fitted a new spark plug.

"Where did you get it?" I eventually asked.

"You don't recognise it?"

"Should I?"

"I don't know. It belonged to a friend of mine's son. He bought himself a road bike a couple of years ago and this has been sitting in their shed."

As Dad coloured in the puzzle of where the bike had come from, I got the feeling I had seen it somewhere before and then it just clicked. It was Amber's brother's bike and I'd seen it on the tour of their machinery shed.

"Ross Jackson," I said and Dad smiled.

"What's going on here?" asked Caitlin, giving Dad and me a fright. I'd thought she was in town.

"Nothing," said Dad. He winked at me.

"Whose bike?"

"Mine." I patted the seat proudly.

"Rubbish!" Caitlin growled. "You can't stop lying, can you, Brad?"

"It's true! It's mine. Dad got it for me from

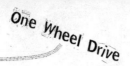

Ross Jackson . . ."

Then she was laughing. So was Dad. Caitlin knew the story. She was just winding me up.

"You be careful on that thing," she said.

"Yes, Mum."

"Well, Mum's not here, is she? Somebody has to say it or it just wouldn't be right."

Dad filled the fuel tank from a jerrycan and helped me wheel it into the paddock. I put the helmet on and tightened the strap.

"Kick it in the guts, mate," Dad said. He was still grinning. Caitlin was standing a little way behind with her arms crossed, staring at me.

"What?" she said.

"Stop looking at me!" I howled.

"Can't even look at my little brother now, hey? What's the world coming to?"

"You just want to see me mess up."

"Me? How can you say such a thing? And so what if I'm watching for the crashes? Isn't that why people watch the car racing?"

I unfolded the kick-starter and gave it heaps. It started third try and the engine lumped and rumbled under my backside. It ran like new.

"Go easy to start with," Dad shouted.

I nodded and toed it into gear, releasing the clutch slowly, but I still managed to spin the back wheel. Caitlin squealed. I imagined her legs getting pelted with clumps of grass and earth. Then I was off, across the paddock, changing through the gears and laughing into my helmet.

Some people like four, some like two, but me, I like one-wheel drive the best.